Beryl's Cove and the Elvis Man

Beryl's Cove and the Elvis Man

By
Janet McCanless

E-BookTime, LLC
Montgomery, Alabama

Beryl's Cove and the Elvis Man

ISBN: 978-1-59824-674-2

First Edition
Published July 2007
E-BookTime, LLC
6598 Pumpkin Road
Montgomery, AL 36108
www.e-booktime.com

To Bob
&
"M.J."

Chapter One

Suzanne Coldwell slid her arm out from under the covers and pushed the alarms snooze button. She just wasn't ready to get up this morning. Tourist season officially opened with the arrival of spring, and there was so much yet to do at the shop, but, after a late night of pizza and video rentals with her best friend, Lorraine, Suzanne wanted only sleep on this morning.

The ringing of the phone wakened her more fully, as she unwrapped all the bedclothes, and made her way over to the computer desk to grab at it.

"Wake up sleepyhead," Lorraine's voice chirped to her. "Have you heard the weather report this morning?"

"Lorraine, I just now got out of the bed, the last thing I want to think about is a weather report." Suzanne ran her long fingers through her auburn hair, and tugged at her drapes to have a look outside. "Why, what's up?"

"Nor'easter is predicted all along the eastern coast, from Myrtle Beach up to New England. Kind of late in the season but they are saying it's going to be a doozy, reckon we'd better batten down the hatches. If I were you, I wouldn't put anything outside that shop of yours that can't be brought in a hurry. We still on for lunch?"

Lorraine Brackett had been Suzanne's best friend since junior high school days, but, sometimes Suzanne got so tired of Lorraine's bossiness and meddling. There was so much to do today, she had a truckload of antiques coming in from New York that had to be unloaded, she needed her flowerboxes repaired, she had an appointment with her attorney to finish the paperwork on the shop, and right now, she just didn't need Lorraine, even if they were best friends.

"I don't know Lorraine, I have so much to do, let's play it, by ear, and I'll give you a call around 11. Right now I've got to shower and get out of here, plus, I need to meet with Jack about 9:30 to complete the paperwork on the shop. Guess it's really mine today. Talk to you later." Hanging up on her friend, she headed for the bathroom.

Two hours later, after a skimpy breakfast and a hot, soaking shower, Suzanne drove down Seabreeze Avenue toward the rustic looking building with the Coldwell Antiques sign atop the doorway. The pansies she had put in the outside planters a few months back were looking a little sad, and she made a mental note to replace them with red Geraniums as soon as she could.

With her key in the door, Suzanne watched as Vern, Beryl's Coves' downtown mailman waved her to a stop. "Mornin Miz Coldwell, seen the weather report?" Thumbing through the mail, he placed a stack of envelopes in her hands. "S'posed to be a humdinger! Comin in late tonight, early tomorrow. Folks down at the marina tying up their boats now, but it'd be better if they rode them out aways and anchored. Won't be bangin up against the dock then." With a wave he was off down the street before Suzanne could comment. Moving into her shop, she flipped on the lights, hung out her open sign, and checked the back for the new inventory that was due in. "Damn that Roger," she thought, as she noticed the new stock piled in the center of the storeroom. Roger Brady had worked for her for about 6 months, and, while brawny enough to move her inventory around, he lacked-a lot of initiative. "Have to tell him every little thing to do," she muttered. She kept a small blackboard in the storeroom where she and Roger left messages to one another, and, picking up the chalk, she wrote a note telling him to uncrate and inventory the new stock, and get out a handful of tags for her to price it all. Then she scrawled that she would be at the attorneys office from 9:30 to 10:00.

Hearing the jingle of bells at the front door, she peeked out from the back room, to see Mildred Jenkins browsing through the shop.

"Morning Mildred," Suzanne came around a corner where she placed some milk glass whatnots on a nearby shelf and walked over to her neighbor. "Looking for anything in particular this morning, or are you just looking?" Suzanne didn't especially care for Mildred, she was, after all, considered Beryl's Coves greatest gossip, but the woman had money, and class. A formidable figure, the wealthy Mrs. Jenkins was not to be ignored.

Feigning indifference, Mildred picked up a few things, always careful to replace them slightly askew from where she had gotten them. Turning over a plate in her hand, she eyed Suzanne. "You met the new man in town?" Heard he's some big time art dealer from Norfolk down here to check out the local real estate. Surprised your friend Lorraine hasn't mentioned him Suzanne. He's a real catch, from what I've heard. You have any Limoges tea cups?" She walked over to where Suzanne was standing and peered over the tops of her glasses at her. "My sister Gladys, why you remember Gladys don't you? Well, it seems she ran off with a local fisherman to Florida years ago. Everybody who is anybody thought for sure they would not stay together. Boy, wasn't I surprised to find out they married, and my brother-in-law runs a charter service. They are doing quite well actually, but we didn't hear from them for years you know. Seems Gladys was a might embarrassed to find she had married beneath her, but all's well that ends well I reckon."

"Hm," Suzanne offered. "You mentioned Limoges? Over here are some nice pieces I just got in from France. I have a set of demitasse cups and saucers Mildred if you are interested." Gesturing towards a table in front of the window, she moved to the cash register, and began putting money in it from her bank bag. "You're my first customer today Mildred, excuse me while I set up here will you? Let me know if I can help you any, hear?"

Looking up, Suzanne saw Mildred holding two demitasse cups and saucers out for her to wrap. "About Gladys," she continued, "these are for her. She always loved them, and Buster and I are thinking of going to Pensacola in a few weeks to visit, and I'd love to bring her these, sort of a peace offering you know. Would you wrap them for me please, Suzanne?"

Shaking her head after the departure of the very eccentric Mrs. Jenkins, Suzanne was surprised to find Jack Miller coming into the store.

Jack was one of four very capable attorneys in Beryl's Cove, although he was the only one in fulltime practice there. He had been attorney to the elder Coldwells, and, following their death, Suzanne saw no reason to change. A small man, he was known as a person of integrity and intellect. Her parents death had hit Suzanne hard, and Jack and MaeRuth had been a strong rock for her as they formalized the terms of the parents will, leaving the antique shop that had operated on Seabreeze Avenue for many years, to their only child and heir.

"Sorry for the intrusion Suze, but I've got to take a deposition this morning, I didn't know I had to do, and, I saw no reason why we couldn't do this here. No point in you coming to the office, when you can sign these right here, it's just a formality anyway."

Clearing a place on the counter for his briefcase, he handed her a pen, and pointed to the paper in front of her.

"Sign here, he said, indicating 2 blank lines. "I'll file these with clerk of court when I'm over in New Bern next week. Beautiful day isn't it?" he added, "but s'posed to be some bad stuff moving in. You doing all right Suze? Everything about to get settled and finalized?" Jack refolded his papers and placed them in the briefcase. "MaeRuth says to tell you hey, and we'd be pleased to have you to dinner real soon. She'll call, that ok?"

"Everything's fine Jack, I thank you for asking, and I'll look forward to MaeRuth's call. I guess this is final then, isn't it? Reckon it's really mine, but I take no pleasure in it. I really thought I would continue to be just the buyer, going here and there, living out of a suitcase. Hope I can run this place as well as Mom and Dad did. Wish me luck, huh?"

"Will do, gotta run now, you be good Suze, and I'll be in touch. Call us if we can be of any help."

Suzanne watched as Jack began walking towards his office. Beryl's Cove was small enough that most everyone walked anywhere they wanted to go in the downtown business area.

Checking her watch, she still had hours to go before meeting Lorraine for lunch.

Chapter Two

Suzanne found Lorraine at a corner table, with a view of the marina. The Captains Table was a trendy little restaurant that was a local favorite. Nautical pictures and a sea going theme gave the place real atmosphere. Once tourist season began, the locals would find it hard to get a table, but today, although busy, it was a few tables shy of being full.

Sliding into a chair, Suzanne gave her friend a quizzical look, "what, is my face on crooked? What are you looking at Rainey?"

Pointing a manicured, polished finger at her friend, Lorraine gave her just a hint of a smile.

"I have found the perfect man for you," she offered, sipping at her glass of white wine. "By the way, I've already ordered the lobster salad for us, I know how you love it."

"My God, Raine," Suzanne sighed, "don't you ever quit? If this man is so great, keep him for yourself, I'm not looking, and what makes you think I want the lobster salad today?"

"First off," Lorraine began," after 2 losers for ex-husbands, I've sworn off men, and secondly, you always order lobster salad in here, you have no life, and what's more, you're in a rut, which is exactly why you need this fellow. His name is Steve Thomas, he's 55, and an art dealer from Norfolk. He's here in Beryl's Cove to find a house.

He's single, good looking, and very rich, in other words, perfect for you."

Swallowing some wine, Suzanne put her glass down and looked at her friend.

"Why?"

"Because you're 50 years old, still good looking, and you need a man Suze. How long has it been since that relationship you had with that traveling salesman?" Lorraine snapped her fingers, "What's his name, Donald?"

"Douglas," Suzanne corrected, "and we broke up by mutual consent Raine, I had my career, and he wanted me at home, barefoot and pregnant. He was just **so** needy, and, quite frankly, I just didn't need that kind of relationship, not then anyway. Oh, I don't know, I've just spent so much time on the road buying, I really just didn't have time for one, and now, I'm not even sure I want one."

Aiming her fork as she spoke, Lorraine smiled and continued, "see, you need someone. How long has it been since you've had sex with anyone?" Lorraine looked up and waved to some friends who had just entered the dining room.

"Lor - Raine!" Suzanne shifted in her chair as her outburst caused several nearby diners to turn and look their way. "My sex life is not open for discussion, thank you very much," she hissed, "besides, you haven't answered my question. Why is this Thomas fellow here in Beryl's Cove?"

Attacking her salad with gusto, Lorraine spoke between bites, "was here 2 years ago for the Fishermans Wharf Festival and thought he'd like to settle here someday. Now that he plans to be semi-retired, he came to the Cove hoping to buy a place. He wants first row though, and I don't have a listing any closer to the water than third row, so, for now, he's living on his yacht at the marina, The Lucky Lady. It's a gorgeous boat Suze, you really ought -to come down to the marina and look him and it over, you might find you're missing something."

Pursing her lips to apply lipstick, Lorraine took a last swallow of wine, "Who knows," she said, "he may be just what you need."

"Well," Suzanne began, "according to Mildred Jenkins he's quite the catch. She was in my store this morning buying teacups for that sorry sister of hers in Pensacola, but if you ask me, she just came in to snoop."

"All I know," Lorraine said, "is you'd better hurry, as he is mooring his boat out in the harbor tonight in anticipation of the storm that's brewing. Have you looked over towards New Bern and seen those black clouds? I saw Jimmy over at the Yacht Club buying plywood for the club windows this morning while I was in the hardware store. Not supposed to be as strong as a hurricane, but definitely a big storm. Guess he can't be too careful with all that glass. And here it is the end of March, and we're having to put up with this mess. Ain't it a bitch too, as I was just getting my summer rentals all lined up." Getting up from the table, Lorraine gathered her purse and was off, waving to other diners as she went. "Thanks for the lunch girlfriend!"

Turning in her chair, Suzanne hollered after her, "Hey, I'm not paying for this!" She looked up just in time to see the waitress drop the check next to her.

"You can pay up front, and have a nice day."

Grabbing the bill from the table, Suzanne muttered to herself, "wouldn't you know it, stuck with the tab. God, I've got to find that girl a hobby!"

Back at the store, she worked all afternoon pricing the things Roger had uncrated for her. Except for a couple of early tourists from the Midwest, store traffic was light all afternoon. She had sent Roger off to the nursery to buy red Geraniums for her flowerboxes out front, she was sweeping out the back room, when the front door bells jangled.

Coming into the front of the store, Suzanne gazed at the most beautiful brown eyes she had ever seen. They were attached to the best looking man she had ever seen. This had to be the newcomer everyone was talking about. Offering him her hand she barely stammered out her name. "S... Suzanne Goldwell, may I be of service?"

"Like the banker," he said, staring into her own brown eyes.

"Excuse me?" withdrawing her hand, Suzanne could not imagine a more handsome man anywhere. Dressed beautifully, everything about him screamed "class", and his blue shirt and tan pants just set off his wonderful tan, and brown eyes. She was mesmerized, and, she had to admit it, everyone was right about this one.

"You know, Coldwell Banker, the real estate firm. Your name's the same."

"Oh, well, I guess I haven't really thought about it much. You're Steve Thomas aren't you?"

Smiling at her through flawless teeth, Steve gave a slight nod of his head. "At your service ma'am, I see the town gossips have been at work."

Suzanne couldn't help the blush that started at her neck and worked its way up through the top of her head. "I'm sorry Mr. Thomas, any newcomer is always grist for the mill around here. Welcome to Beryl's Cove. How may I help you?"

"I need a ships bell. Someone at the marina said that yours was the best antique store in Pykes County, and that if anyone had a bell, it would be you. I had one, but somehow or other it has gotten cracked. You do have one don't you?" Steve spent several moments taking in the antique store. It seemed to meet with his approval as his gaze returned to Suzanne.

Picking one up from the shelf, she handed it to him. "I have 2 or 3 I think, and this seems to be a popular size. It needs a rope pull, but I can get one put on for you easy enough."

Their hands brushed one another as they exchanged the bell. Steve gave her an impish grin that spread into a broad smile. "If you could get it fixed up for me, I'd appreciate it. Why don't you bring it down to the marina, I'm in slip 9, The Lucky Lady. I'm taking her out to anchor in the harbor this afternoon, how soon can I expect you?"

"About an hour," Suzanne told him.

"Watching him leave the store, she was surprised to find herself trembling. She watched until Steve was out of the store and headed back towards the docks at the marina.

An hour later, after Roger had attached the bell pull, Suzanne threaded her way along the wharf looking for slip 9. In the short time since Steve had left her shop, the storm clouds had gathered and darkened, the wind was picking up, and the temperature was dropping fast. Fishermen were reeling in and packing up, leaving the pier fishing for another day. Coldwell Antiques was only four doors down from the marina, and Suzanne was there in under a minute.

Stopping in front of the slip, she noticed Steve working amid the lines. The Lucky Lady slapped at the wake as she rolled gently in the water.

"Ahoy there," he called to her. "I was just getting ready to go and ride out this storm. Welcome aboard!" Steve came around to where she was standing and offered her a hand climbing aboard. Taking the wrapped bell from her arms, he asked, "Care for a quick tour?" Taking Suzanne's elbow, Steve guided her below deck to the salon.

Below, Suzanne tried to take it all in, and, raising her eyebrows, she said, "This is beautiful, how big is she?"

"65 feet. Good sized, but not a monster. I wanted something I could captain myself. How do you like the color scheme?"

"That's what I was looking at," she said "I love it, did you do it yourself?" Suzanne couldn't take her eyes off the bright, pumpkin colored salon chairs, and the carpeting was a sturdy, industrial weight oatmeal and sand Berber. She walked around the large salon, noticing the artwork, the corner bar, and the brass lamps. On the wall, behind the bar was a portrait of Elvis Presley. She studied it awhile and moved to sit on one of the chairs. "It's quite striking," she added, "and looks very comfortable."

"C'mon," he said, helping her up, let me show you the master salon and the galley. I'm a gourmet cook, you know.

Smiling that broad smile of his, he guided Suzanne around the boat, then led her towards the steps leading to the upper deck. "It's my home away from home," he said. "Someday I'd love to take you out in it, but not today. Today, I need to get her underway and get anchored out in the harbor. I have a buddy who's taking a small motor boat out to bring me back to shore. Maybe you could tell me if there's a hotel or a nice inn around town where I can stay to ride out this storm?" He looked at her with those big, liquid eyes, and, before she could even give it some thought, Suzanne Coldwell threw caution to the wind, and did the most impulsive thing she had ever done in her life.

"Um, you know, I have a guest room that is never used, you could stay with me. The storm won't last long, and I'm sure you'd be comfortable, and, umm, I could fix us a nice dinner, or you could fix dinner if you want, and, gosh..." Suzanne paused to take a breath, and was aware that she was babbling, something she did whenever she got excited. "Oh my God," she thought to herself, "if Lorraine Brackett could just hear me now. No life, she says, well, Rainey, I've just made a liar out of you!"

Laughing, Steve looked at her. "Well, if you're sure, I promise not to be any trouble. Tell you what, ride with me, just out into the harbor, and we'll be back in no time, then we can be on our way. What do you say?"

It seemed no time at all before they were back at the marina, The Lucky Lady safely moored in the harbor. After a quick trip to the antique store to lock up and secure the shutters, Suzanne and Steve hopped into her Nissan, and drove the two blocks down Eventide Lane to the Coldwell cottage. It had begun to rain as they passed all the quaint and rustic cottages that dotted the area. Suzanne's house sat midway between her antique store and Lorraine's real estate office on Oak Ave. Her house could be seen from Raines office window, except in late spring and summer when all the trees were leafed out. Thank God for all those trees Suzanne thought, as they were beginning to get full now, and the last thing she wanted her best friend to see was her running into the house with the handsomest man to ever set foot in the cove.

Racing inside, they managed to close the front door just as the rain hit with full fury. The sky darkened, and all of Beryl's Cove hunkered down, for what was sure to be an adventurous night.

Chapter Three

After securing the house and garage, Suzanne and Steve fixed a supper of salad and omelets. While she did the dishes, he built a fire.

"You never know when one of these freak storms is going to knock out power," he aimed his remarks toward the kitchen, as he piled 2 logs on top of the newspapers and kindling. "Better to be safe than sorry. Boy, listen to that rain, will you?" he offered as he returned to the kitchen area. "Isn't it unusual to have a storm like this so late in the season?"

"No, not really." Suzanne finished with the dishes, dried her hands, and led the way back into the living room. Taking a seat on the sofa that faced the fire, she put her feet up on the ottoman. "This has really been a strange winter, and the spring doesn't look any better so far. It should be a lot warmer than it's been, for instance, and, we should have more flowers blooming than we do. I sure hope the cold temperatures don't affect the tourist season, we all depend on it so." Rising, she walked over to the bar and poured 2 glasses of Chardonnay. Bringing one to him, she resumed her seat on the sofa. "Tell me about yourself Steve. Where's your art gallery?"

Turning a club chair around to face Suzanne, he sat down on it, sharing the ottoman with her.

"Waterside. You know," he gestured around the room, "I love this house, very cozy, not filled with all those nautical and beach doo dads. The chintz in here is truly fabulous, and, I must say Suzanne, your art work is very interesting."

"Hm, thanks, I have an aunt in Durham who is an artist, and she does most of my paintings. I sell a few of her pictures at the store when I can. Waterside? I didn't know that place had a good art gallery in it. I've always thought it was just a mall full of glitzy junk."

Setting his wine down on a small, round, table, Steve leaned forward and gave one of those throaty laughs she was beginning to find quite endearing.

"Elvis," he said.

"Excuse me?"

"Elvis, velvet and otherwise. I have one of the largest collections of Elvis Presley memorabilia on the entire East Coast. You really should see it sometime. You saw the portrait on the Lady.

"Elvis Presley?" Suzanne couldn't believe what she was hearing. "Are you serious, you really deal in Elvis stuff?"

"Yes, indeed, it's quite a lucrative field," Steve countered. "Hell, somebody has to make money off the stuff, it might as well be me! Here," he pulled a key chain out of his pocket. Dangling from the chain was a small, plastic figure of Elvis Presley, wearing a pink jacket and black satin pants. Across his shoulders was draped a pink guitar. "Look," he offered, "I'll give this to you, just as a keepsake, it's one of my top sellers."

Suzanne could hardly believe what she was hearing. She didn't know whether to take the key chain and be flattered, or insulted. As she watched the Elvis figure dangle at the end of the chain, she had a hard time finding the words to continue their conversation.

Seeing her discomfort, Steve continued. "Oh, I know Lorraine's telling everybody, including you when she had lunch with you today, that I'm a wealthy art dealer from Norfolk. Well, I'm from Norfolk, of course, not originally, but when I got out of the Navy, after 30 years, I just stuck around. I had saved some money, so I bought a little shop at the Waterside complex, but, hey, it keeps me off the streets, and you would be surprised at how many folks are really into Elvis. People flock to buy his memorabilia." He looked at her, smiled, and moved onto the sofa beside her. Pulling a small catalogue from his hip pocket, Steve began thumbing through it, finally offering it to her. "I carry a full line of merchandise, here, look for yourself."

Suzanne was speechless, trying to take it all in. She continued to stare at her guest with a mixture of puzzlement and disbelief.

"You said Lorraine told me this at lunch today. How did you know that?" She was becoming uncomfortable with this line of conversation, and, it was beginning to dawn on her the full extent of her friends meddling.

"Wellll," Steve too, was getting a sense that the evening wasn't going the way he had hoped or planned. "Lorraine's trying to find me a house here, and, well, you know how she talks. She really likes you Suzanne, and well, she just felt you being a lonely spinster and all that we could..."

"Lonely spinster??? What in the hell are you talking about? The two of you! You set me up, didn't you.... well didn't you?" She was beyond angry, she was furious. Mad at Lorraine for her infernal meddling, and mad that this man considered this encounter a "sympathy meeting". Mad at herself for not seeing it coming. Most of all, she was mad at the weather, because it was too bad to throw this creep out of her house!

"No, I ah... You don't seem to understand, it's not..."

Getting up from the sofa, Suzanne glared at her guest. She returned her wine glass to the bar, and moved toward the staircase. "This conversation is over Steve, in fact, this night is over. Your room is down that hallway on the left, the bath is across from you. I'm going to bed now, and, as soon as this storm is over, I expect you **out of here.** And that can't come too soon for me. Goodnight!!"

She started up the stairs, when Steve called after her. "What about the fire?" He asked.

"You built it, you put it out!" She shouted from the top of the staircase.

The last thing he heard was her bedroom door slamming shut, and the lock being put on.

Chapter Four

Suzanne slept fitfully through the night and the storm. Wind gusts blew heavy limbs down, upturned trash cans, and scattered debris everywhere. She had tossed and turned, ranted and raved, and railed against her friends' interfering in her life. Determined to have it out with Lorraine, soon after going upstairs, she had called her, but the storm had made the connection too noisy and full of static, and too dangerous to be talking on the phone for any length of time. They had briefly agreed to meet the next day at the Dry Dock, the cocktail lounge at the opposite end of Seabreeze Avenue from the marina. When she woke at 6 the next morning, it was to an extremely bright and clear day.

Although she lived 2 blocks from the ocean, Suzanne had a good view of the water from her upstairs bedroom window. Gazing out at the harbor, she found it hard to believe that such a raging storm could be followed by this degree of calmness and beauty. A phenomenon she felt was peculiar to the North Carolina coast.

Emerging from the shower, she stood in front of her closet towel drying her hair, and hoping against hope that Steve Thomas was long gone from downstairs.

Selecting a pair of tan gabardine slacks, and a brown plaid shirt, she dressed for the work she felt lay before her this day, straightening out the mess she knew her shop would be in.

Promptly at 8, after breakfast and a quick sweep of her guest room, Suzanne opened the front door of Coldwells Antiques. The fractured front planters lay in shambles on the sidewalk, the red Geraniums she had just had Roger put out were spilled out everywhere. While everything in the front showroom area looked intact, she made her way to the back, wondering just what she might find,

There, disaster had clearly struck. She assumed the storm had blown her back door open, as she waded through mud and debris. Some porcelain vases and statuary lay in pieces on the floor, covered in wet mud, and a number of lamps sat lop-sided on the shelves. Papers everywhere, overturned baskets, and broken china and crystal littered the floor and shelves. She was heartsick as she made her way through all the broken and shattered pieces of her life. She bent and picked up a small, brass clock she knew had been in a box on the top shelf of the closet. "How could it now be on the floor," she wondered. Running both her hands through her hair, she was determined not to cry, like some school girl, and she set about making an inventory of the damage to give the insurance company. Hopefully Roger would be in soon to lend her a hand.

Arriving at 8:30, Roger assured her that he had secured the back door when he had left the night before.

They worked silently for several hours restoring order to the shop, both front and back. It was sometime after eleven when they heard the bells over the front door. Suzanne went into the front to see Kevin McLaughlin standing just inside the door.

Kevin owned and operated the hardware store that was three doors down from Coldwells Antiques. Tall, in his mid-thirties, Kevin was a sweet man whom Suzanne was enjoying getting re-acquainted with. When she left Beryl's Cove, to travel as a buyer for her parents, Kevin was away at college.

Well known locally, his hardware store was a going concern in town.

"Kevin, hey, what brings you in this morning? Do you know you're the only person who has set foot inside my door so far today? Guess cleanup has everybody pretty busy, huh."

"You're right about that Suze, the main road that leads out of town, and towards the interstate is blocked. Seems that huge tree that was in Sam Meyers front yard came down last night, so no one can get in or out of town, at least for now. Crew's working on it now, and they should have it cut up and out of the way by one o'clock or so. That's the reason no one is in the shops this morning. Nobody but locals here cept the few folks that are put up at Mildred Jenkins' inn up the street."

Nodding, Suzanne walked over towards the cash register, and picked up a rag which she wiped her hands on.

"Interesting, I had no idea. That tree was a landmark, and virtually the biggest one around here. What in the world is Sam going to do for shade I wonder. What brings you in?"

"My back door was open this morning, naturally, everything was a mess, but I'm missing some things, and I wondered how you all have fared."

"What kinds of things, Kevin?" Suzanne asked.

"Well, stuff that had been packed up in boxes is all over the floor, and, when I tried to take an inventory, I noticed I'm missing a bunch of odd ball stuff, a huge sledge hammer for one, and, it seems hard to believe a storm would open boxes that were in a closet, and that hammer weighed a ton. I just don't believe the rain and wind came in and swept it away. I think I was robbed and it was made to look like something else."

Approaching him, Suzanne pointed at him with the rag still in her hand. "You know, I've had the same thing happen here. There was a clock I know was in a box in my store room closet, and this morning it was on the floor. Near as I can figure, Roger and I are missing some old yardsticks, a pair of scissors, and an old shovel we kept around for our gardening projects. Strange huh? Oh, and my back door was open as well, but I just assumed it was due to the storm."

Kevin backed up to the door, opened it as if to leave, and turned around to face Suzanne. "Just what I suspected. I'm going next door and see if the Brown sisters have had any damage or vandalism to the flower shop. If I hear anything, I'll let you know, then, we'd better go see Chief Morgan. I think we have a thief operating in town Suze, See ya!" He was out the door, and in the flower shop in a matter of seconds.

Glancing at the clock, Suzanne realized she had fifteen minutes to get up with Lorraine at the Dry Dock. She hurriedly washed her hands, splashed water on her face, ran a comb through her hair, and told Roger to put the closed sign out. She'd be back in thirty minutes she told him.

Walking quickly down Seabreeze Avenue, she traveled the 2 blocks to the Dry Dock in record time. Too upset to be hungry, Suzanne reasoned she'd have a quick glass of tea, tell off the indomitable Ms. Brackett, and return to her shop, all in a half hour. The walk would do her good, she reasoned, besides, she needed the exercise.

The Dry Dock was full. Always dimly lighted, the place was bustling with locals talking about the storm. Buster and Mildred Jenkins were at a corner table nursing Bloody Marys and club sandwiches; at another table sat Karl Stevenson, now the owner of the old Coldwell Mercantile Warehouse and Fishery. The business had been started and owned by Suzanne's grandfather. Following his death nearly twenty years ago, her father, Melvin, had sold the enterprise to Karl. He had come down the coast from Delaware, liked the area, and settled down. He was looking for a business to buy, so the timing was right, as Melvin Coldwell did not possess the business acumen to operate the factory, despite having spent all his formative years at the warehouse helping his father. Melvin was interested in antiques. So far, Karl had continued the success of the senior Coldwell, and it was because of him that all the local fishermen were able to find an outside market for their catch.

She nodded to Karl, and waved to the Jenkins as she took a chair at Lorraine's table.

"This won't take long Raine, you and I have to talk!"

"Well, hello to you too," Raine pouted as she checked her make-up in her mirror. "Want to know where I've been?"

"Yes....no!" Suzanne blurted, "We have to talk, Just tea," she ordered from the waiter.

"Just tea? For heavens sake eat something." She stopped the waiter by grabbing his arm, then adding, "She'll have the club sandwich."

"Rainey, stop! This is what we have to talk about, your incessant meddling! You, girlfriend, are a busy body, a pain in the ass, and you are fast making me regret that I ever came back here. Now about this Steve Thomas thing........"

Lorraine interrupted, "have you met him yet, isn't he the most gorgeous guy you've ever laid eyes on? When was the last time you had any contact with the old crowd Suze? How about Phyllis? You know she was married to Jeff Wagner, but, he died here about three year ago, and she married a nice guy, what's his name.........Mike! Mike O'Neill. Some kind of chemist with one of those pharmaceutical plants at the Research Triangle area. They live in Cary I think."

Exasperated, Suzanne sighed. "If they live in Cary, how am I supposed to have contact with her? And what does this have to do with the fact you are an incorrigible busy body, and I don't need you planning my life this way Raine, I really don't."

Lorraine put her sandwich down and dabbed at her mouth, "Oh pooh, Suzie dear, you have no life. Going all over the world like you did, did you ever once get out of your hotel room or go somewhere else beside a stuffy old warehouse, or see the sights, or have an affair, for Pete's sake!"

"Lor-raine!" Suzanne hissed, "You have no idea what I did in my off hours." Angry as she was, Suzanne felt even worse, knowing her friend was right. She had made some disastrous choices in men, maybe Raine was right, perhaps she really didn't have much of a life.

"Oh Raine"

Placing a hand on her friends arm, Lorraine began again. "Suze, I'm just trying to help. You were gone such a long time. My God, you finished school, and then, zip, you disappeared, and I had no one to talk to when I went through my divorces. It's so good to have you back home. I just want to make certain that you're happy, and enjoy yourself. It must have been awful losing both your parents within so short a time. They were such incredibly decent people," she added. "It's me, Raine, your oldest and dearest friend. I want to help." Patting her arm, Lorraine turned her attention to the couple who had just walked into the pub. Smiling and waving, she tapped Suzanne on the hand and nodded in their direction.

"It's them," she whispered. "That's where I've been. They are Mark and Jean Roberts. He's an orthopedic surgeon from Burlington. They're moving here to be closer to his parents in Baylors Point. I've been showing them property last night and this morning. Isn't it exciting, a new doctor in the area, and Baylors Point is only four miles down the road, and their marina isn't nearly as nice as ours, which means, they'll be joining our Yacht club and spending money in Beryl's Cove. By the way, she's looking for some really fine antiques for the new place, so I've told her about your store. She'll most likely be coming in soon."

"That's wonderful, really. What do they plan on buying over at Baylors?"

Finishing her tea, Lorraine set the empty glass down, and winked at her friend. "Well, we're looking at a couple of places; they should make a decision by the end of the week. Now, tell me about your encounter with our hunky Mr. Thomas," she leaned towards her friend. "I'm all ears."

Looking intently across the table at her best friend, Suzanne pushed her plate away. For several moments she said nothing.

"Raine, I'm fifty years old, I truly do not need you to choreograph my life like this, AND, I am NOT a lonely spinster like you told Steve. Really, I'm quite happy with my life."

Curious, Lorraine eyed her friend, "are you going to tell me about your encounter with him or not?"

"We met briefly, yesterday, when he came in to buy a bell, which I suspect, you put him up to. What in the world were you doing out in that storm last night?"

"Well," Lorraine explained, "it wasn't really last night, more like afternoon. Soon as I left you, as a matter of fact. I took them to Baylors Point, the storm was coming up, so we headed back. They stayed at the Sandpiper Motel, and me, getting back just before you phoned last night. Boy, that was some storm, huh? Blew open my back door, and dislodged my file cabinet and stuff, and, I have got to find one of my computers, guess the high winds just carried it away."

Suzanne picked up her handbag, threw enough money on the table to cover the lunch, plus a tip, and grabbed Lorraine by the hand, bringing her to her feet.

"Hey, what're you doing, where are we going in such a rush?"

"To chief Morgan's. There's something blowing around here, and it's more than a wind. Get your purse Raine, you're driving!"

Chapter Five

Everyone else, it seemed, had the same idea. When Lorraine and Suzanne got to the police department, half the store owners were there. Kevin McLaughlin was holding forth, with the Brown sisters in tow. Judy Wagner, who owned the dress shop was waiting her turn with the chief, as was Clyde McMartin, proprietor of the Beryl's Cove Bait N Tackle shop. They had all been vandalized it seems, and their back doors left open to the storm.

There were a bunch of people converging in his office to complain all at once. The line of citizens at Alices' desk was fairly long, and, the undercurrent of conversation pretty loud, driving the chief to get up and leave his office, heading for the break room. Enjoying a cup of coffee, he was just beginning to feel a little bit less tense, when the dispatcher at the front desk walked in looking for him.

"Need you up front chief," he said.

"What's the trouble Mike?" Chief Morgan followed the younger man to the front office, bringing his coffee and a hastily grabbed Danish with him.

Standing in front of the chief were the Brown sisters, octogenarian twins who owned the flower shop on Seabreeze Avenue. Each of them stood before the chief clutching their matching handbags, and each with a look of distress on her face.

"Ladies, afternoon Miz Edna, Miz Harriette. What can I do for you, Alice get your statements all right?"

"Oh yes, chief," It was Edna, speaking for both of them, as was her usual custom. "But, Harriette and I got to thinking, with all these strange goings on just since the storm, we'd forgotten to tell you about something we should have mentioned a week or more ago." The two sisters eyed each other, and both nodded at the other one, almost in unison.

"You see, our shop is directly across the median from the Murdoch Mansion, and well, we kind of notice things that go on in that direction."

"We can't help but see Chief, after all, we spend a good deal of time in the front, and, well, the house practically takes up the whole block..........." Harriette chimed in.

"Yes, yes, ladies, please, go on."

"Well," Edna continued. "About ten days ago we noticed that the care taker was no longer coming in over there every day like he had been doing for years."

"That's right!" Harriette nodded, "Years."

"Anyway," Edna explained, "We didn't pay it too much attention, but Harriette and I couldn't help but notice that in the past week, the place has taken on a particularly deserted look.....almost like it had been abandoned."

"Abandoned," Harriette added.

"Well, Chief, we just thought maybe the old guy was on vacation, but then, that terrible storm came up, and the grounds over there are looking especially beat up today, and, still no care taker. Well, my goodness, we just knew we had to say something." Edna let out a deep sigh, glad she had gotten it all out.

"Yes, say something," Harriette offered. Both sisters looked pleadingly at Chief Morgan, hoping he could resolve what was obviously, to them a big problem.

Setting his coffee and Danish down on the nearest desk, Morgan wiped his hands on a hankerchief, then taking each sister by the arm, he escorted them to the door. "I am so glad you came to me with this girls," he liked to refer to the 82 year old twins as girls, it delighted them, and earned favor for him. A little schmoozing of the old folk never hurt, he thought to himself. "I'll get an officer over there to have a look see, now, you two sweethearts run on along. Get back to that flower shop of yours and work your magic with those lovely blooms you have. I'll let you know if anything turns up. Thanks for coming in."

The chief sat back down at his desk just as the last statement was being dictated to Alice. Rubbing his chin, he felt as if he had worked two shifts, just since the morning, what with trying to clear the seven block downtown area of all the debris from the storm, the reported thefts and vandalism; Sam Meyers trying to get the town to pick up the cost of clearing that huge old water oak away, and, now, this.

Two more years until retirement, he thought to himself, just two more years!

When the last person had filed out of the police station, the chief grabbed his cap and headed out the door. Nodding to Alice, he told her his plans. "Going to check some things Alice, and before I head home, I'm going to check out the Murdoch place. Just to have a look see. You can get me through dispatch, I reckon." He was out the door before the secretary could reply.

Easing his car through the streets and alleys of the Beryl's Cove business district, the chief noticed all the tree limbs and debris everywhere. City crews were out trying to clean up, but it appeared every house and business downtown had had some storm damage. Litter was everywhere, and, as he drove east to west on Seabreeze, he waved to Suzanne and Roger who were piling the splintered flower boxes and some wet, muddy crates at the curb.

Stopping in front of the Murdoch Mansion, he saw the yard was littered with several large tree limbs; a couple of shutters were missing, and there was a screen or two flapping away from its frame.

The house was huge, three full floors, plus a basement. Old man Murdoch had practically built the downtown area. His house and the Coldwell Mercantile building were the oldest structures in Beryl's Cove. The Murdoch family had moved to the cove in its earliest days. Mr. Murdoch had had the good sense and foresight to realize that the area was perfect for tourism, and set about building up the town. Eventually, all the families' holdings were sold to the individual merchants, giving the old man the money to start up the marina and yacht club. Nine generations had lived in the homeplace, each one putting their own individual stamp and style on the house. It had always been alive with parties and gatherings, and, in its day had been a virtual showplace. About six years ago, the last known member of the Murdoch family had died, leaving the care of the house to a trust fund. The administrator of that fund paid for a full time care taker. The house and grounds had been maintained, with the idea that as soon as a sponsor could be found, the home would be made over into a cultural center. Perhaps a place to showcase local crafts and talent. In six years, no sponsor had been found so the custodian continued with his daily work.

Pulling off the street onto the gravel driveway, Morgan turned off the ignition, and got out of his patrol car. All but two acres of grounds had been sold off, so, he set about to walk all of it. Tossing aside sticks, twigs, and smaller limbs, the chief stepped off the sodden yard, his feet sinking oftentimes into puddles made by the previous night's torrential rains. Walking around the back of the house, he noticed the cellar door standing open. Approaching, he shone his flashlight down into the darkened basement, hollered a loud "halloo"; saw and heard nothing, so he surmised the storm had blown the door open. Slamming it shut, and hooking it from the outside, he continued to walk around the other side of the house. Finding nothing but a storm-littered yard, Morgan made the decision that all was well, and that sooner or later, the errant groundskeeper would return. Arthur Morgan returned to his patrol car and headed home.

On the third floor of the mansion, a shadow moved across the window, and a pair of deep-set eyes watched as the police car made its way down the street.

Once the car was out of sight, the man in the shadows moved away from the window. Taking his time in the dark house, he made his way cautiously down the wide, once elegant staircase that wound its way down and around to the main floor. Quietly moving across the room, he went into the kitchen area, feeling his way along the wall until his hand rested on the doorknob of the entrance to the cellar.

It was only when he had closed the door behind him and he could smell the dank basement, did he use a dim flashlight to make his way down the steps and over to the corner of the cellar where he laid down on a dirty mattress, where he slept, waiting for the darkness of night.

Chapter Six

The week after Easter brought the first heavy influx of tourists to the Cove. Lorraine's summer rentals were all leased for the season, and the Seaside Inn had the NO VACANCY sign out. Mildred and Buster Jenkins made a quick trip to Florida to see Gladys, only to return with her after a week. Gladys took up residence at the Inn, and was helping out however she was able, she didn't speak of her marriage, or her reason for returning to Beryl's Cove, and no one else did either.

Sam Meyers got his fallen tree removed, at his expense, and Steve Thomas, along with all the other boat owners, had long since returned to the marina, and, en masse, they spent the better part of each day polishing, scraping, or in some way maintaining the boats.

Steve's and Suzanne's paths hadn't crossed since the night of that fateful storm, but, he thought of her nearly every waking hour. He stayed in touch with his gallery by phone or fax, and continued to look for just the right place to buy.

Suzanne, Kevin McLaughlin, and the other merchants hounded Chief Morgan about a suspect in the vandalism and thefts that sprang up following the storm. Small things here and there continued to disappear from many of the stores so Kevin and some of the men from the Bait N Tackle formed a community watch program to try and catch the thief, but to no avail. Small acts of vandalism continued, and it was discovered that someone was stealing food from the Captains Table, and, the caretaker for the Murdoch Mansion was still away, causing the Brown sisters to fret more with each passing day.

It was about 10:00 on a Wednesday morning, when the bells over Suzanne's door jangled. She came out from behind a bright, yellow, Victorian settee, to see Jean Roberts browsing around the shop.

"Mrs. Roberts, what a nice surprise! Have you gotten settled in Baylors Point yet? What can I help you with today?" Suzanne moved this and that as she spoke, hopefully, not too eagerly.

"Call me Jean, please." Jean Roberts was immaculately groomed, in a beige, silk, pantsuit, Hermes scarf, and strippy sandals. Her blonde hair was tied at the nape of her neck, and she looked every inch the wealthy doctors wife. "Yes, thank you, we bought that big, glass fronted house right on the water, do you know it? Lorraine said it used to be owned by some movie star. Anyway, she told me yours was THE place to shop, and, until now, I've not had the opportunity to come in. We've been trying to hire staff, that sort of thing." She picked up some pretty Majolica, admiring the bright colors. "You have some lovely pieces here, but I'm particularly interested in a nice pair of buffet lamps, and perhaps some artwork for the dining room."

Suzanne showed the woman around the store, pointing out items here and there she thought the Roberts' would like. Jean ended up with the lamps, a lovely 20" by 24." floral oil painting, a Queen Anne wing chair, and a pastel Aubusson area rug. The total came to well over $3500 as Suzanne rang up the purchases.

"I'm certain you'll be pleased with all of these Mrs. Roberts....Jean, and I'll have Roger deliver them right after dinner. We truly do thank you."

Walking towards the back of the store, where she would give Roger his delivery instructions, she picked up a Baccarat crystal bowl which she added to the order, as a complimentary house warming gift.

Putting Roger to work, she picked up the phone, and dialed Loraine.

Kelly, the secretary, answered on the first ring.

"Brackett Real Estate, Oh hey Miz Coldwell, yes she is, hold on, and I'll connect you."

"Suzanne!" Lorraine gushed. "How nice of you to call. We've not gotten together in almost two weeks now, when are we going to do lunch again? I promise to be good!"

"Raine, I just sold a huge order to Jean Roberts, and she paid in cash. I want to celebrate. Let's eat supper at the yacht club tonight. What do you say, about sevenish? I'll call over there and get us a reservation. See ya later!"

"Whoa, hold on a minute, what's the latest with you and your boy friend, Steve?" Lorraine was an incurable gossip, and wanted nothing more than to hear some juicy story, especially if it concerned her long-time friend.

"You'll never change, will you?" Suzanne sounded exasperated. "I'm in too good a mood to let you spoil my day for me. Haven't heard a thing, and **no,** he's not my boy friend. Now, remember, you promised to be good! Till later, bye."

No sooner had she hung up from the club, and turned around, when in walked the subject of the day, Steve Thomas.

"Hey," he said, standing directly in front of her. "Mind if I come in?"

"Looks to me like you are already in Mr. Thomas. "What can I do for you?"

"Um, look, seems we got off on the wrong foot the other week. Since the night of the storm, I've been awfully busy keeping up my boat, and doing some work at my laptop. I just needed to "take a break, and I wondered how you were." He didn't say anything more, and neither did she. They simply stared at one another like smitten school children.

Suzanne finally found her voice. "I'm fine, no serious damage to the store, a lot of mud and water, and some packing cases tossed about. Of course, my flower boxes in front need to be replaced, but nothing major. How about you?"

Steve moved a little closer towards her, he could have touched her had he wanted to, and he definitely wanted to. "Uh, well, as you know, I want to settle here, at least for part of the year, and, I know so little about the town, I was hoping maybe you'd take me around, you know, sort of walk all over town and point out people and places to me. How about after you close. 5:30 is it? And please, call me Steve." He hoped he did not sound as desperate as he felt.

Suzanne really felt sorry for him. Maybe, she thought, she had been too hasty. What would it hurt to take a walk?

"Ok, Steve," she began, "but I'm meeting someone for supper at seven, and I had planned to use the time between closing and then to sort of freshen up, but, I think I'd really like to take a walk with you and show you the town. I have to be at the Yacht Club at seven though, understood?"

"I do," he answered. "Suzanne, you really don't need to change or freshen up at all, why I think you look wonderful. A striking resemblance to Marlo Thomas, but I guess you've been told that before."

Smiling broadly, she grabbed her handbag, and left a note for Roger on the chalkboard. Returning to the store front, she seemed very pleased to be going somewhere with Steve. "Yes, I have been told that, but I don't see it myself, but of course, I love the compliment. It's not quite closing, but let's go anyway. We'll take a right on the sidewalk, and take in the town from one end to the other, and, hopefully, wind up at the Yacht Club at 7:00."

The two of them headed west on Seabreeze Avenue, with Suzanne pointing out any and everything she thought would be of interest to Steve. They passed the Murdoch Mansion, but didn't see the eyes staring out at them from the third floor, nor the cellar door barely hanging on its hinges. She did notice the broken windows, and made a mental note to tell Chief Morgan about it when she saw him. They walked past the Coldwell Mercantile and Fishery, all the town, with Suzanne giving a thumbnail history of each place.

As they turned at the traffic circle heading east again, she pointed out Sam Myers place, explaining that his mini-warehouses were further out of town, on the road to Baylors Point.

The pair strolled past new homes being built on the bluff behind the Inn; the refurbished Town Hall, and the new fire truck and the small library in the back of the municipal building.

It was 6:45 when they stopped in front of the Yacht Club entrance.

"Well," Suzanne said, "here we are, anything else you want to know?"

My God, Steve thought, but she was beautiful. He did not want the evening to end. Glancing at his watch, he remarked, "We still have 15 minutes until your dinner date, have a drink with me?"

Shifting her handbag from one shoulder to another, she brushed his hand briefly, then headed towards the club. "Sorry, I really have to go. Some other time?"

"Yeah, sure, I'll take you up on that, and thanks for the walk. I enjoyed it!" Steve was virtually breathless as she disappeared inside the club. Thrusting his hands in his pockets, he set off down the boardwalk to the Lucky Lady. He felt ten years old and like a million bucks!

While she waited for Lorraine, Suzanne ordered a white wine, and sat, very relaxed, gazing at the water. There was just something so soothing about watching tranquil water. There was little boat activity this night, and, from somewhere on the marina a radio played a slow love song. The club dining room held over a hundred people, but tonight, business was slow, and Suzanne did not recognize any of the other diners. Must be tourists, she thought. Taking her eyes off the water, she spied her friend making her way across the room to their table.

"Hi," they both said at once. Lorraine took the menu from the waiter, and stared at her friend. "What are we having?"

Suzanne appeared mesmerized by the water, as she was completely oblivious to anything Lorraine was telling her.

"Hey," Lorraine poked her in the arm, "Yoo hoo, I'm over here!"

"I'm sorry Rainey, the water just seems to be so hypnotic tonight. What were you saying?"

Lorraine folded her menu, and placed her napkin in her lap just as the waiter appeared with her drink, "Uh huh, don't you think I can tell you are hooked; girlfriend, you got it bad! So, tell me, how was the walk, quiet and romantic, or your regular history lesson?"

Suzanne shot her friend a glaring look, but Lorraine put her hand up, as if to silence her. "Now don't go getting huffy on me Suze, everybody in town saw the two of you strolling for the last hour and a half. This is a small place, you can walk it end to end in about 20 minutes, so, you must have been enjoying yourself. Really, you make a handsome couple. When are you going out with him?"

"Crab cakes."

"S'cuse me?" Lorraine was dumbfounded by her friends strange behavior.

"You asked what we were having, and tonight, **I'm** doing the ordering. Crab cakes, and no, haven't made a date yet. Not only that missy, I won't tell you about it if and when I do. New, tell me how goes the real estate business?"

Suzanne sat at the table, pretending to be interested in Lorraine's real estate business, but all she thought about was Steve Thomas. She made a stab at eating the crab cakes, but, in the end, she merely pushed them around on her plate.

The women lived across the street from one another, and both had walked the two blocks to the club, so, together, around ten, they walked each other home. Climbing the stairs to her bedroom, Suzanne paused at the window on the landing, for one more glimpse of the ocean. The night was beautiful, warm, and starry, and here she was, acting like a school girl. She made herself a mental note to give herself a stern talking to in the morning.

The phone was ringing somewhere, and, Suzanne had to come back to reality to answer it. The clock on her bedside table showed it to be 10:45. When she said hello, she realized that Steve was on the other end.

"Sorry to call you so late Suzanne, I, uh, just wanted to make sure you had gotten home all right." He sounded genuinely concerned, and, he was not about to let her know he had been calling every 15 minutes for the past three hours, hoping to catch her before she went to bed.

"Thank you, I'm fine. I appreciate your concern, but it is late, you know."

"I know." He did not want this conversation or the evening to be over. "Listen, there is this man, an Elvis collector, and he wants to meet me in the lobby of the Blockade Runner in Wilmington on Friday. I'll be with him probably for several hours, all afternoon maybe, so, I may end up staying over. Would you like to come with me? It might be fun, and I'm sure there are antique dealers in town you could call on."

Suzanne couldn't stop herself, she accepted Steve's offer. She would go to Wilmington with him....for the night, and she would probably do something she would very much regret later.

Chapter Seven

Friday morning, bright and early, Chief Morgan met Suzanne at the door of her shop. Keys at the ready, she was just about to enter, when the chief appeared, as if from nowhere.

"Mornin Suzanne, I wonder if I might have a word with you, inside," he nodded towards the interior of the store, as they moved inside.

"What is it chief?"

Shuffling his feet, hat in hand, he looked down at the floor. "Well, I need to speak with this fellow Steve Thomas. Would you ask him to come to my office as soon as possible?"

Totally mystified over Morgan's request, she shrugged her shoulders at him. "Chief, what makes you think Steve is here, in my shop, for heavens sake. He's not here, he's over on his boat, The Lucky Lady. Go down to the marina and ask him yourself if you must. What's this about anyway?"

Running his hand through his thinning hair, Morgan continued. "Ma'am, Mr. Thomas' boat is no longer at the marina, and hasn't been in several days now, and, I was told, he was staying with you."

Suzanne had to sit, before she fell down. "Well, you were told wrong. He's...., he's not with me chief, and I couldn't fathom a guess as to where he has been, or is now. I'm supposed to see him around 1:00 this afternoon. I'll be glad to give him the message."

Chief Morgan left Suzanne sitting on a chair in her store front. Her gaze was fixed, and her emotions, raging. She had no idea why he would be wanted by the police chief, and, more importantly, where was his boat, and him? Roger came in and found his boss sitting statue-like in one of her matching rocking chairs in the window of the store. He began a conversation with her, and, after several seconds, realized she was not responding to him. Moving over to her, he nudged her shoulder. "Hey, Suze, what's the matter?"

"Oh Roger, I don't know. Chief Morgan was just in here looking for Steve Thomas. No one knows where he is, and his boat is not at the marina, hasn't been for days, so he says. I just saw him two nights ago, and he didn't say anything to me about leaving town, at least, not in his boat." Suzanne looked stricken.

Roger Brady was a newcomer to the Cove, having just gotten out of the Army a year ago. He drifted up the coast from Florida, looking for work, and not succeeding until he happened upon Suzanne one day in the hardware store. It turned out Roger was a distant relation of the McLaughlins, he sought them out, in the hopes of some kind of a job, when Suzanne came into Kevin's store. She overheard their conversation, and offered him work. He'd been in Beryl's Cove ever since, living in the small apartment over Kevin's hardware, and loved it. What he lacked in initiative, he made up for in his fondness for Suzanne, and he was developing a real knack for the antique business. Suzanne trusted him. Kneeling in front of her now, he took her hands in his. "Suze, why don't you wait until you see Steve, there may be a really logical explanation for it all. I've seen him around town the past few weeks, and he seems like a really nice guy. Why don't you just come right out and ask him? You might be surprised."

Sighing, she looked into Rogers eyes. "You're right of course. Why am I like this, it's almost as if I'm afraid all the time that everything that is good in my life is going to be snatched away. I'm such a pessimist, and, right now, I'm acting much too immature for my age. Of course I need to give him the chance to explain things, but, you know, Roger, it's really none of my business is it? The chief probably just wants to ask him something about all these thefts that keep occurring. Lawd, I wish Morgan would catch the guy, this business has me completely unnerved." She got up and headed towards the back room where she would put her handbag for the day, and where she geared up for business each day. "Have you had time to notice if anything is missing today?"

"No, it doesn't look like anything's gone. Let me take a quick look around the storeroom. Be back in a flash."

Suzanne glanced at her mail while she listened to Roger move boxes and furniture in the storeroom. She heard a loud thud, and saw Roger coming out shaking his wrist. "I dropped a fairly large box on my foot, and when I went to move it, I twisted my wrist in a funny angle. I think it'll be okay though. Don't think anything's missing. Any interesting mail?"

Since coming to work for her Roger had shown a lot of interest in the shop, and seemed to possess an uncanny marketing ability. She had let him create some ads for the local paper, and they proved to be really good, garnering a lot of interest in her antiques.

As she hung the "OPEN" sign at the door, Suzanne noticed Clyde McMartin moving at a fast pace across the street, and heading straight for the police station two blocks away. Not thirty seconds later, Judy Wagner left the dress shop and headed in the same direction. They both looked fit to kill. Suzanne hoped that whatever the problem was, it would be settled quickly. Surely, it couldn't be more thefts, they had just about stopped, at least none of the merchants had mentioned any more in the past week. Sighing audibly, she turned her attention to getting her merchandise dusted and made presentable for the day ahead. Steve was supposed to pick her up at 1:00 in the afternoon, and, until that time, she decided, she would just concentrate on selling antiques, nothing more.

At 1:00 sharp, Steve walked into Coldwell Antiques, put his canvas sports bag down on the floor, and found Suzanne behind a new credenza she was going over with a polishing cloth. She hadn't heard him come in, but was certainly glad to see him. Giving her a gentle peck on the cheek, he asked her if she was ready to go.

Smiling up at him, she nodded, and went back to find Roger and give him instructions for the remainder of the day. "I'll be back early tomorrow most likely Roger, so go ahead and open up, and I'll be along. You know, Wilmington's just an hour or so down the coast, so we won't be back late. Oh, and if that 0"Reilly woman comes in for her package, it's on a shelf in the storeroom, marked fragile. You can't miss it."

Roger smiled at her, waved to Steve, and told her to get "the hell outta Dodge". "Go, have a nice time, and don't worry about a thing!"

Out on the street, Suzanne looked up and down Seabreeze Avenue, finally turned to Steve and asked, "Where's the rental car you said you'd have?"

Sheepishly, he shrugged his shoulders, laughed and told her "don't have it. I had to go to the Seaside Inn to reserve it, and that Jenkins woman promised she'd have one for us, but this morning, guess what, no car. Reckon we'll have to take yours, do you mind? I can buy your gas for you," he offered.

Suzanne felt those old doubts welling up inside her again. Knowing this man was like being on a roller coaster, she thought, as nothing seemed to be as it should with him.

"No, I guess not. Do you mind walking to the house, it's only two blocks, and we'll have to stop and get the gas."

They crossed the street, towards Eventide Lane, and headed for her house'. "Did Mildred say why she didn't get the car?" she inquired after a brief lull in conversation.

"Nope, just said they couldn't get one here before morning, and I'm meeting with Ben at 4:00 today. Couldn't wait. Listen, if you're not comfortable with this, we can make other arrangements. I'll call Ben and ask him to stay over another night so we can meet tomorrow. I think if he had to, he would."

"No, that's okay." Suzanne picked up the pace somewhat and headed for her garage. "I've left an overnight bag in the front hall, and I'll go and grab it. You can go to the car, it's unlocked, so go ahead and get in, I'll be there in a jiff. Don't feel you need to wait here for me."

Steve filled up Suzanne's car on the way out of town. Buying her gas, he jumped back into the Nissan, and they headed towards Coastal Highway 17, and Wilmington.

They were both pensive for several minutes, Suzanne wondering if she had done the right thing, Steve contemplating how he was going to tell her what he had to tell her. Finally, they both spoke at once, each saying the others name.

Laughing, Steve bowed his head in her direction, insisting that she go first.

"No, really," Suzanne smiled, "please, you first."

Steve looked out at the beautiful scenery, just as the North Carolina Department of Transportation truck passed them. Division of Highways was printed on its side, and Steve seemed', to want to think about his words, as he waved to the men in the truck.

"Um, well, I feel foolish asking you to do me a favor, after imposing on you with your car and all. Especially since that awful night when things just seemed to go badly for us, but, well, here goes. Could I ask you to sort of keep messages for me? Seems my boat is in drydock, and I'm over at the Sandpiper Motel, and, well, if someone should want to see me or want to know where I am, could they leave messages with you at the shop? I'll check in with you each day, so I'm hoping you'll agree to this. Oh, by the way," he continued," Chief Morgan saw me this morning, so you don't need to tell me he's looking for me, I've already spoken with him."

Much to Steve's surprise, Suzanne was laughing, and giving him the biggest grin he had ever seen on her face.

"What, what's so funny?" he asked her.

"Oh nothing, I'm just glad you've asked me this, Of course someone can leave a message or contact you through me. Don't give it another thought, and, boy, am I glad we're taking this trip together. Steve, you just don't know how glad!" Suzanne just couldn't stop grinning, and Steve, although rather confused, grinned right back at her.

They were both beginning to relax and enjoy the short trip to Wilmington. Finally, Steve turned in the seat to face her.

"Hey," he began, "I know a lot about you, but you've not asked many questions about me. Isn't there something you'd like to know about me? Go ahead, ask me anything."

Smiling at him, Suzanne tried to watch the road, while not taking her eyes off the gorgeous Mr. Thomas. "Well, all right, what did you do in the Navy?"

"Intelligence work, Naval intelligence. Anything else?"

"O.k., any family?"

"Parents dead," he began. "My father died in the Korean War, and my mom raised me and my older brother Eugene. He's out in Oregon someplace, I haven't seen or spoken to him in years, simply because we have gone our separate ways for so long. No hard feelings, just no feelings at all I guess. Reckon we'll get together one of these days. Now it's my turn," he continued. "I know you lost both your parents last summer, was it an accident?"

"No," Suzanne said, "old age. They simply wore themselves out in the shop. I was their buyer, going all over, I didn't get home much. Haven't lived in the Cove full-time for twenty years. Oh, I'd be home every holiday, and maybe for a week or two here and there, but that's pretty much it. Another question for you."

"Shoot."

"Who runs your Elvis show for you while you are semi-retired?"

Steve had to laugh at her terminology. He had never heard his memorabilia referred to as an "Elvis Show". He ran his hand through his silver hair. "M.J."

"Who is M.J.?" she wanted to know.

"My partner, M. J. Follett. Bought a half interest in the place, which is great, cause it allows me to travel, look for a house in Beryl's Cove, and add to my collection, while M.J. minds the store back in Virginia. We stay in touch by fax and PC. I'm really grateful to old M.J., I couldn't do this without my partner."

"What did he want?" Suzanne asked.

"Who?"

"Chief Morgan. What did he want?"

Steve laughed, he was beginning to catch on to Suzanne's way of speaking in non-sequiters. "Well, being in Naval Intelligence, he thought I could help him catch this thief who is operating in the Cove. We shared some ideas. Oh, by the way, gonna be a big meeting of the shop owners in the chief's office on Monday night. A few of the boat owners too, at least the ones who have been hit. A little brain-storming, see what we can come up with. Are you in?"

"I'm in," she fairly shouted in her glee. "By the way, Steve Thomas, why aren't you married?"

"Because, Suzanne Coldwell, I never stayed in one place long enough to get caught. You?"

"The same," she replied, still with a big grin on her face.

They cruised down highway 17 towards Wilmington. Not saying much, just happy to be in one another's company.

Chapter Eight

Dropping Steve at the Blockade Runner, Suzanne went on into the downtown area, promising to meet up with him back at the hotel at six. He went on in to register for them, take the bags up to the rooms, and prepare to meet his friend. It was decided that they would meet in the cocktail lounge at six for drinks, then, have dinner, and a nice, romantic evening before heading back to Beryl's Cove on Saturday.

Suzanne parked and, getting out of her car, she walked towards the ocean. A warm, salty, breeze blew through her, hair, and she sat on a bench in the sun for several minutes, before retrieving her briefcase and heading towards the antique mall across the street. It was time to go to work, and she hoped to finish in plenty of time to meet Steve in a few hours.

Returning to the hotel early, she went to her room to shower and change for her evening. Choosing a simple turquoise shift she knew would look spectacular with her dark coloring and long, slender legs, she took the elevator to the main floor, and found her way to the lounge, which was right off the lobby.

Suzanne was nursing a glass of white wine, when Steve came in with another gentleman.

"Suzanne, I want you to meet a fellow Elvis dealer, Ben Alexander. Ben, this is the mighty Suzanne I've been telling you about."

Ben shook her hand, and took a seat opposite her at the table. Steve sat down next to her, and motioned for the waiter. The two men sat there grinning at her, when finally, Steve said, "don't you notice anything strange about Bens name Suze?"

Giving him a quizzical look, she shook her head.

"Ben Alexander," the man said again. "You know, the actor who played opposite Jack Webb in the original Dragnet series. The actor's name was Ben Alexander."

Failing to ring any bells with her, Suzanne was, nevertheless, gracious. "I'm sorry, Mr. Alexander, I'm afraid I didn't see that one. My family wasn't much on TV watching. It was probably before my time anyway. It is nice to meet you though. Have you known Steve very long?"

Slapping his knee, Ben gave a hearty laugh. "Boy, Thomas, you've sure got a keeper in this one! Young lady, you are a jewel! Did anyone ever tell you that you look like Marlo Thomas?"

Suzanne smiled at Ben, nodded, and, before she could add anything, he continued. "Listen, I want you and Thomas here to come out to Vegas sometime and see my Elvis museum. We got a fella there who does a mean imitation as well. You'd love it Margo, and, you could take in the sights. Our "Elvis" does two shows daily, and, he's quite a hit. Ever been to Vegas Maria?"

Suzanne was vigorously nodding her head, while looking pleadingly at Steve. She had never met anyone like the gusty Ben Alexander, and, she couldn't help the feeling, that surely he was kidding with them.

After a quick drink Ben left the two of them, and they proceeded to the dining room for dinner. Steve made the remark that she looked more than beautiful, and, she noticed that he looked awfully good himself.

Dinner was delightful and leisurely. Following the meal, they moved to the patio beside the pool. A few couples strolled the beach that night, and there was one other party of four enjoying the evening on the other side of the patio area. The air was not yet laden with the mugginess that summers brought to the coast, and the honeysuckle was out in force, giving the night a lovely fragrance. A little bit of a breeze was wafting their way from the ocean that sat mere yards from them. Somewhere, probably the ballroom, an orchestra was playing "Strangers in the Night."

Settling into the wrought iron chairs, Suzanne became pensive as she gazed at the sparkling water.

"A penny for your thought," offered Steve.

Smiling at him, Suzanne eased back in her chair, and gave him a deep look. "Your friend Ben is quite a character. Is he for real?"

Laughing, Steve pulled his chair closer to hers. "What do you mean, for real, you met him, you spoke with him. He's a mess, isn't he?"

"He called me young lady. Does he have any inkling of how old I am?"

"No, probably not. Ben must be seventy, seventy-five at least. And, you should know that age is irrelevant. Do you feel any different than you did when you were a teen-ager? I sure don't."

"I was never a teen-ager Steve," she told him. "I've worked nearly all my life, but, no, I don't feel any different I guess."

"Tell you what, you need some fun and spontaneity in your life, want to dance?" He was in front of her, holding out his hand as she rose.

"You mean, here, now?"

"Why not," Steve said. "Listen to that wonderful trumpet, and "Strangers in the Night" has always been one of my favorites." In no time, his arm was around her and they swayed to the music, right there, next to the pool.

After several minutes she pulled away from him. "Hey Thomas, the music's stopped." Her eyes fairly sparkled as she looked at him in the moonlight.

Steve brought her to him again, as his arm went around her waist. Gently, they danced, even though there was no music. Inside the ballroom, polite clapping from the revelers, as the band started up its next song, a lively fast number, that neither Steve nor Suzanne recognized.

They danced every dance that night, until well past midnight. The moon and stars were out, and the two of them simply did not want the evening to be over. They were the only ones out now, and, gradually, they came to a stop, and Steve walked over to where they had been sitting, picked up Suzanne's purse for her, and, taking her hand, they headed for the elevator.

On the second floor, they stopped in the middle of the hallway. Steve's room was on one side of the hall, hers on the other. Bringing her hand up to his lips, he gently kissed it, and gave her an inquisitive raise of his eyebrows.

She was breathless, but managed to find her key in her handbag. She gave it to him and whispered, "My room."

Just before closing and locking the door, Steve hung the "Do Not Disturb" sign on the knob.

Outside, lovers came from several of the areas restaurants and clubs down to the beach for a. late night stroll, and schools of Dolphins jumped and cavorted in their evening play. That night, Beryl's Cove, or anyplace else for that matter was the farthest thing from anyone's mind.

Chapter Nine

Suzanne awoke Saturday morning to bright sunlight streaming into the room. Shaking her head to clear it, she looked around for Steve, and found him on the balcony, gazing at the ocean. Slipping into a robe, she joined him at the table. He was pouring coffee from a room service tray, and, he handed her a cup.

"Mm," she purred. "You really are too good to be true. Do you do this for all your 'amours'?" She sipped her coffee, and gazed contentedly at him.

"Nope," he replied, "just the ones who drive their own cars to the rendezvous. Sleep good?"

"Unbelievable!" She was so refreshed, she told him. "You're just what the doctor ordered. Now what?" Finishing her coffee, she reached for the pot, and refilled both their cups.

"I think, Coldwell, that last night makes us an item, a 'thing', a significant other to each of us. What d'ya think?" He smiled that wonderful smile of his, and reached for her hand.

"You are the only person," she said, "whose life reads like something from a sitcom. Knowing you is like being in a time warp."

"Oh, how so?"

"Well, for one thing, you have a brother named Eugene in Oregon, you know a man named Ben Alexander, and you dance when there is no music. I've never known anyone like you. You can't be real, oh yes," she added," You have a partner named M.J."

He smiled, and kissed her hand. "I also went to school with a kid named Darren Stevens......."

Simultaneously, they pointed to the other and said, "The husband on Bewitched!"

"Did I mention," he went on, "that I deal in Elvis memorabilia? Now, will you go steady with me?"

Suzanne fairly roared with laughter, as she set her coffee down. "Go steady with you?"

"Yeah, go steady," Steve looked like a bad little boy, with his rumpled hair, and stubbly face. She hoped she never tired of looking at him.

Walking over to him, she sat down in his lap and laid her head on his shoulder. "You bet your ass!"

"Good," he said, "Now, we have one more thing to do before we head home." He picked her up like a small doll, and walked inside the room with her, where he shut the sliding glass door, and closed the drapes.

Chapter Ten

Suzanne walked into her shop Saturday around lunch time. She and Steve had showered, dressed, and checked out of the Blockade Runner by 10:30, and were home in Beryl's Cove by one. Pulling into her garage, they took in their bags, and agreed to meet later at the Yacht Club for dinner. She walked the two blocks to the antique store, and walked in just as Roger was ringing up a sale.

"Hey Boss," he chirped, coming around the counter to greet her. "Did you have a nice trip?" He grinned at her in a particularly impish way.

"You behave yourself," she admonished him, "or I'll have Kevin put you in his basement and throw away the key!" she playfully shook a finger at him. "Yes, I had a lovely time, now, tell me what's going on."

"Well," Roger, began, "Mrs. O'Reilly came after her package, and I just now sold that Japanese credenza we got in about a month ago. They'll pick it up themselves on Monday morning. Oh, the most important, boy, did we have some excitement yesterday, right after you left! Seems Clyde McMartin and Judy Wagner were both robbed sometime Thursday night, and just before you left, they had gotten a note, each of them, in the mail, telling then there would be more thefts and vandalism unless the merchants agreed, en masse, to stop pandering to the tourists. Caused quite a stir when they went into the chief's office to complain about it."

"I can imagine, but Roger, not trading to tourists is crazy, this town was founded and developed for tourists. It's how we all make our living. What kind of a person would demand that we stop? That would effectively kill our livelihood, and town?"

"I agree Suze, but, they both got notes on Friday, and Chief Morgan has been talking to everybody in the whole downtown area since. He'll probably be here to talk to you and Steve before the sun sets. " Roger left the showroom area, and went to the back of the store. He came out with the morning's mail and handed it to Suzanne.

Engrossed in the mail, she did not hear the bells jangle, or even see the door open, when, suddenly, she looked up and saw Lorraine standing in front of her.

"Well, I'm waiting, "Lorraine teased. "Now don't tell me it was nothing, everyone in town saw the two of you leave together, so, out with it babe, tell me everything, I want details!" Lorraine pulled up a Bentwood rocker and sat facing her friend. Motioning for Roger to leave the room, she looked expectantly at Suzanne.

Grinning back at Lorraine, Suzanne just shook her head. "No way," she said. "I told you I was not going to be forthcoming about this. Let's just say that we had a nice time, and, we're going steady."

"Going steady?" Lorraine fairly hooted. "Tell me you are kidding! People our age don't go steady."

"Well," Suzanne laughed, "we are. Now, scoot, I've got work to do."

Just as Lorraine was going out the door, Chief Morgan was coming in. Tipping his hat at Lorraine, he approached Suzanne. "Afternoon, Miz Coldwell. Roger tell you the happenings of yesterday afternoon?"

"Yes, he did chief. When are you going to start calling me Suzanne, like a friend? Miz Coldwell makes me sound so old." She walked over to the cash register as she spoke. "I'm afraid I can't help you though, I haven't a clue as to what sort of an individual is doing these things. I just know it must be as upsetting to all the merchants, as it is to me. How about the Brown sister, have they managed to escape this thievery?"

"Well," Morgan began, "Mis Edna says they haven't missed anything but some ribbon, and heavy twine, but, of course, Miz Harriette thinks everybody's life is in danger. She is absolutely certain that a mad dog killer's loose in the town, and, she is convinced the missing care taker for the Murdoch Mansion has something to do with it. What I need from you, is for you to tell me where I can find our Steve Thomas."

Suzanne looked up from her invoice book at Chief Morgan. "Well, I expect he's on his way over to Bradshaws landing and Dry Dock, to check on the progress of The Lucky Lady. You can probably find him over there this afternoon."

Returning his cap to his head, Chief Morgan waved to Suzanne, and was out the door. He got into his patrol car and headed over to the landing, which was located on the other side of the private beach that fronted the Seaside Inn.

Suzanne hollered to Roger that she was going next door to the flower shop, and she was out the door, and in the Brown sisters store, just as Miz Harriette was coming out the door with the floral arrangements for the church. "Ooh Suzanne," she was almost breathless. "Sister's in the back, do stick around, I'm going to run these over to the Mariners Chapel, and be right back. I mean right back, Go on in."

"My goodness, Suzanne," Edna had a tendency to gush over her fellow tradesmen. "My, but you're stunning this afternoon, and, I'm told, you have a new beau. How exciting. Really, you should sit down here, and tell me all about your new fella. Is he nice?"

Suzanne had to laugh, the two sisters always seemed like they were from another age. A new beau indeed. Smiling, she looked into the clear blue eyes of Edna Brown, and simply nodded. "Oh yes, Miz Edna, very nice, and he'll be good for Beryl's Cove too. I'm not here to talk about him though, I want to know how you and Miz Harriette are faring during all these thefts."

The two ladies sat in garden chairs that decorated the floral shop. "Oh my," Edna began, "you know, this is scary business. When it was simply stealing and vandalism, it didn't seem so bad, but now, there have been letters sent. You know, sister and I haven't lost that much, some ribbons we would have put on sale anyway, and a ball of twine. I guess right after that bad storm, we were missing some garden tools, and a step ladder, but nothing much since. It's just that Harriette is so worried, you know how she frets so." Taking hold of Suzanne's hand, Edna Brown teared up as she continued. "It's just that........well, you know if anything happened to either of us Suzanne, I just don't know how we would cope." She shook her head side to side, and looked helplessly at her friend.

Suzanne patted the woman's hand, "now, don't you worry Edna, nothing is going to happen to either of you. Chief Morgan is right on top of this. Are you still convinced that the missing caretaker is the key to all this?"

"Oh, absolutely! Just can't put my finger on why, but it all seems so suspicious, him being gone, and then all this going on. That place is a landmark, and it shouldn't be allowed to fall into such disrepair like it is. Such a pity. The Murdochs took such good care of that place, didn't they?"

"Yes ma'am, they surely did." Suzanne got up to leave, and gently touched Edna Brown on the shoulder. "You just hang in there Miz Edna, we'll catch the guy. Don't you and Miz Harriette worry about a thing."

"Thank you Suzanne, you are such a good girl, I'll tell Harriette when she gets back. In the meantime, I think I'll keep our doors locked anyway, and, oh, one more thing, I still want you to come by and tell us about your new beau, and bring him along," Edna called after Suzanne, who was already out the door and standing on the sidewalk.

"Will do, and yes, keep those doors locked," she shouted as she reentered her own shop.

Suzanne spent the rest of the afternoon waiting on an influx of tourists. The last one left at 6:00, and, she reasoned, she had just enough time to get home and change before meeting Steve.

Chapter Eleven

They sat at a table in the area of the dining room that jutted out right over the water, but Steve and Suzanne had eyes only for each other. They waved to the other patrons, and several stopped to chat. They were looked on as a couple now, and even Lorraine seemed content just to see the two of them together, although she told everyone in town that it was she who had arranged it all.

Following a leisurely dinner, Steve led Suzanne by the hand as they made their way down the steps toward the beach. Walking along the sand, they heard no sound except for the boats quietly rocking at their moorings. A beautiful night, quiet and serene, and full of stars. After walking a ways, they sat on the seawall, and Steve put his arm around her.

"You know," he said, after a pause, "this going steady is kinda fun, don't you think?" Taking her hand in his he brought it up to his lips and kissed it, ever so gently. "I sure am glad I came to Beryl's Cove, aren't you? Oh, by the way," he said, brightening, "I got an E mail from Ben today. Want to know what he said?"

Smiling at him, Suzanne wrapped her arms around him, and put her head on his shoulder. "Mmnn, very nice, and yes, I am very glad you came to Beryl's Cove. And, what's more, I'm so happy to be going steady with you." Then, she threw her head back and laughing, she looked him in the eye with that curious, wide-eyed look she had. "You are something else again Thomas," she said.

"How so?"

"You and your going steady, I feel like a teen-ager. Do you know that Lorraine told me that people our age should not go steady?"

He raised his eyebrows, and gave her a quizzical stare. "And why is that Coldwell?" wrapping his arm around her more tightly, he pulled her to him.

"Well," Suzanne began, "she thinks we are too old. Reckon she just thinks we should start living together and simply call ourselves partners. Who knows what Lorraine thinks, or why. She needs something more to do with her free time besides meddling in people's lives. She is so pushy, sometimes I really get irritated with her. By the way," she straightened up, and moved slightly away from Steve. "Just why did you zero in on me, so to speak. Did Lorraine put you up to buying that bell, and get you to meet me?"

Steve laughed. "Do you think you are so unattractive that the only way you can appeal to a man is through sympathy? Well, my dear, you are wrong. Actually, I saw you walking down the street while I was sitting in Lorraine's office several weeks ago, and we are talking many, many weeks here. I asked who you were, and she filled me in. She wanted to know if I wanted an introduction. I was absolutely stunned by your beauty, still am, as a matter of fact, and yes, I really needed a bell. Satisfied?"

"Mmnn, yes," she snuggled on his shoulder again. "Good, what did Ben say?"

"He said to tell Margaret hello for him, and hopes we'll see him in Vegas someday."

They both convulsed in peals of laughter, and started back up the steps towards the yacht club. Walking hand in hand, they started for Suzanne's house on Eventide Lane. "Tell you what Coldwell," Steve said.

"What's that Thomas?"

"What say we retire to your house, and discuss our future, and that idea you friend had about living together."

They stopped on the sidewalk briefly before going into the house. The night was so lovely, Steve told her, that he just didn't want to go inside yet. He scanned the horizon, and stopped suddenly, turned to her and whispered, "Suze, look over there, towards the Murdoch place. See it? Looks like a faint light glowing in an upstairs window."

Suzanne strained to see, finally saw what looked like a candle glowing, and looked at Steve. "We'd better tell the chief!" As she turned to go in the house, Steve grabbed her arm.

"No! He doesn't seem to be doing much, I'm going to check it out. You go on up to the house, I'll be back after while."

"What, are you crazy? Steve, you can't do that, I won't let you! It's much too dangerous, what if there's someone in there?"

"Look," he offered, "I know what I'm doing, I'm just going to snoop around a little, whoever's in there is not going to know I'm even around."

"I don't care, you're not going, at least not without me!" She was determined, and wanted him to know how she felt.

"Don't be silly Suze," but he saw the look of determination on her face. Hesitating, he ran his hand through his hair, and looked once again at the Murdoch Mansion, with its dark, shadowy outline against the night sky. Frustrated, he shrugged his shoulders. "Ok," he said, "but you can't go in that flowered dress. How long for you to change?"

"A flash," Suzanne said, running towards the house, "you won't even know I'm gone," she shouted, as she disappeared inside.

"Right," Steve mumbled to himself.

Chapter Twelve

Dressed all in black, and wearing dark shoes, Suzanne followed Steve to the back gate that led to the rear of the Murdoch Mansion. Steve was wearing tan Dockers and deck shoes, but hoped his dark red polo shirt would blend into the night. He was hoping to keep a low enough profile, that he would not be noticed.

Keeping to the shadowy portions of the expansive lawn, the pair worked their way to the cellar door, which opened to the outside. The night was a bright, starry evening, heavy with the scent of honeysuckle and jasmine.

The cellar door had been unlocked since Chief Morgan had been by several weeks before. Steve opened it slowly and peered into the blackness that was the Murdoch basement. Taking a moment for his eyes to adjust to the darkness, he put a finger to his lips, took Suzanne's hand, and ventured into the unknown interior depths of the house.

Once inside, they very cautiously made their way down the three steps into the cellar. Gripping Steve's hand tightly, Suzanne couldn't help the shudder that passed through her body. "This is creepy," she whispered.

"I know, but I think I have a flashlight pen here in my pocket. Wait a minute." Letting go of her hand, Steve patted all his pockets, finally bringing forth a small penlight. He shone a circle of light downward, that enabled them to inch their way across the floor.

"What are we looking for?" Suzanne barely whispered.

"Don't know," Steve answered, "but we'll know when we find it."

Shining the small light all around the cavernous space, Steve found nothing against the walls that would show this to be anything but the basement storage area of a large, abandoned, house.

Aiming the beam of light over one area after another, the furnace, across the room came into view. Running his penlight top to bottom, then bottom to top, Steve stopped it about the halfway point. "Look over there, Suze, see that pile of stuff?"

"Just barely, maybe we should shuffle over there and have a closer look," was her suggestion.

Hand in hand, they carefully made their way towards the furnace.

His light now fading, Steve shone it onto the pile of things he saw. When he did, Suzanne gasped, "Look!" directing his hand over another way, Suzanne was horrified, "there's Lorraine's computer, and look," she said as she pointed Steve's hand in yet another direction, There's Kevin's missing sledge hammer, and I wouldn't be surprised if that was the Brown sisters step ladder. Steve, it's all here, all the things that have been taken. All this other stuff probably belongs to the various other merchants and boat owners. But how did they get here, and who........?"

Steve silenced her by placing a hand over her mouth. "Sh, listen."

Faintly, they heard the sound of footsteps on the floor above them. Heavy footsteps, walking back and forth right above their heads.

Their light almost gone, Steve silently motioned to her to follow him across the huge room, and to the door.

Gripping his hand so tightly it made hers ache, Suzanne was grateful it was too dark for Steve to see the terror in her eyes, terror that she felt with every fiber of her being.

Accidentally scraping against a chair, it went over, making a sharp, splintering sound. "That does it," Steve whispered, "hurry Suze, let's go a little faster, but carefully."

It was then they heard a door open above them, and a beam from a flashlight began scanning the basement.

He had no idea where they were in the cloying darkness, or how far from the door. His light was all but gone, and the darkness of the space very disorienting. He hoped Suzanne had enough presence of mind to stand still and say nothing. He still had a hold of her hand, which, by now, was moist with nervous perspiration. They made no sound as someone made their way down the steps, shining a huge flashlight all around the basement.

Steve surmised that it was a man, judging by the heavy sound of the feet, and fairly tall, considering the angle of light. Steve Thomas was a good-sized man himself, but, in no mood to physically tackle someone he guessed to be well over six feet tall and more than likely heavier than two hundred pounds.

Literally holding her breath, Suzanne listened as the man paced around the basement, shining his light over everything. She had no way of knowing what Steve was thinking, but she hoped he was considering a way out of here.

The man shone his flashlight on the basement door, and Steve saw, to his amazement, they were only about eight feet away, and a little to the right of it. If the man moved his light just a little, he and Suzanne would be revealed to him. Hoping the element of surprise would delay any reaction from the man, Steve stepped forward, squeezed Suzanne's hand, and shouted, "Now!" as the two of them sprinted toward the still illuminated doorway.

Steve was up the steps and out into the moonlit back yard in a flash. Turning back, he saw that Suzanne was not behind him. She had stumbled on the bottom step, fallen, and knocked herself out cold. She lay in a heap on the basement floor, her temple bleeding profusely where she had hit the concrete step.

Before he could reach her, the man in the basement sprinted up the steps, pushed Steve over and was running across the lawn, headed towards First Street, and the alley behind the Coldwell Mercantile, Warehouse, and Fishery.

All of Pykes County, which included Beryl's Cove, Baylors Point, and Pykes Bay was served by Mariners Memorial Hospital, located halfway between Beryl's Cove and Pykes Bay. Fortunately, each town maintained a satellite clinic for the benefit of injured and seasick tourists, and the Beryl's Cove clinic was one street over from the Murdoch Mansion. It and the drugstore occupied a third of a building that was shared with the fire and police departments, and the municipal offices. It was to that 24 hour clinic that Steve carried Suzanne.

Ringing the night bell, he was admitted and led back to an examining room where he placed the now semi-conscious, Suzanne.

The doctor on-call wasted no time cleaning up her temple, shining a light in both her eyes, and numbing the temples so he could stitch it up.

Steve was distraught as he watched from across the room. Every time that needle pierced her skin, he winced.

Finishing up, the doctor removed his gloves, and helped Suzanne to a sitting position.

"I think we'll keep her here tonight, so we can monitor her, but come morning, and Miss Coldwell should be able to return to her home. Probably with a slight headache, but no worse for the wear." The doctor smiled at both of them, and motioned for the nurse to help get Suzanne into one of the beds in the four bed clinic. At this time, she was the only patient, so Steve hoped she would get good care.

He waited until she was in bed, and comfortable, before going into the clinic area to see her.

"How do you feel Coldwell?" he bent and gently kissed her cheek.

"I'm fine, a little woozy, and my head throbs, but I understand that will disappear after about 24 hours. Steve, you need to find Chief Morgan, and tell him what we found. What about that man, who is he?" Suzanne closed her eyes, but kept her hand in Steve's.

"I know, but I hate to leave you. That man, whoever he is, ran away, and I know the chief needs to find him. I have no idea who he might be, you?"

"No." She was getting drowsy, and she knew she would be asleep in a matter of seconds. "I'll be all right darling, go and find Arthur Morgan. I'll be fine, really."

"Oh my God," Steve jumped up from the chair he'd been sitting on, and stared down at her. "You called me darling!"

Smiling, and with closed eyes, Suzanne nodded ever so slightly. "If it bothers you, I won't."

Laughing, Steve kissed her hand, "not on your life," he said, "darling is great, just great."

She was asleep before he left the room to search for Chief Morgan.

The town of Beryl's Cove had insisted that their police chief reside inside the city limits. Since he didn't know the chiefs address, he reasoned that that fact narrowed his search somewhat. At that late hour, there was no one he could call to find out, he would have to search for him alone. Lots of people lived in town, but, except for the merchants, like Suzanne, a great many of them were seasonal. Sam Myers had a big house behind the Mariners Chapel, and, a few folks, like the Kevin McLaughlin family, lived in a new development, Ocean View Estates, between the Coldwell

Mercantile, and the Post Office. Nice, upscale homes; nearly all the home owners were locals who worked year round in the Cove, or they were wealthy, retired folks, there because they enjoyed the ocean, fishing, and good dining that had been a part of Beryl's Cove since its settling, back in the early 1800's.

Steve knew the Morgans did not live in one of the cottages that dotted the area between Suzanne and Lorraine's houses, nor did he occupy one of the Brackett summer rentals. That left only the cluster of townhouses on the bluff beside the Seaside Inn. He set out to walk the two blocks to the area, and see if he could locate the chief. Looking at his watch, he saw that it was after midnight. He hadn't realized how long they had been at the Murdoch place, or the clinic. When they left the yacht club, it had been 9:30.

The Harbor View Townhouses had been built in the early 80's, to accommodate the influx of people wanting to relocate to Beryl's Cove. They were attractive, two story homes, surrounded by lush foliage, with a common area in the back, along with a swimming pool and tennis courts. Twelve homes in all they had been fairly modest in price, and kept up in pretty good condition. The salt air had rusted out some of the outdoor lamps, and the window casements all looked in need of a coat of paint, but otherwise, the complex was in fairly good shape. Steve did not want to knock randomly on doors, so he tried reading names off mail boxes. He got lucky on the tenth one. There, the names Frances and Arthur Morgan were clearly printed and, there was even a light on over the door. He rang the bell.

It was several minutes before the chief opened the door, just slightly, saw Steve, and opened it wide.

Morgan was tying his bathrobe, but ushered his visitor inside. "This better be good Thomas. Come on back to the den, so we don't wake Frances." He lit a cigarette, offered one to Steve, who refused, and sank into his recliner. "Sit, what's on your mind?"

Steve related all that had happened that evening, and everything that he and Suzanne had found in the basement of the Murdoch house. He described the man in the house as being heavy-set, and, at least six feet tall.

"Well," Chief Morgan finally stirred from his chair, walked to the bar, and poured a splash of whiskey in a tumbler, gave it to Steve, then poured one for himself. He reclaimed his recliner. "That fits the description of Lester Pruitt, the caretaker of the place. What he's doing with all that stolen merchandise is a mystery, but it sure doesn't look good does it?"

"I figure he stole it," Steve offered. "Who is this Pruitt fellow anyway chief?"

"Well, the original Mrs. Murdoch, Eleanor, was a Pruitt by birth. Something tells me he's some kinda kin. I need to get with my computer on Monday, and look into that aspect much further. Anyway, maybe he's pissed off about the town going commercial instead of remaining a sleepy little fishing village like the old man intended."

"Chief, I had heard that the older Mr. Murdoch founded the town for tourism." Steve finished his drink, and held out his glass for a refill.

"Oh, he did. But I don't think he intended it to be the main industry. The man was cultured, highly so, liked the arts, that sort of thing. I s'pose he wanted to see more arts than we have. But Steve, we're small, with limited funds, and, no one in town is really qualified to get this arts thing up and running. I mean, we make our living off the tourist trade, plain and simple.

"Suzanne could do it."

"Mmnn, yes, I s'pose she could at that. Well, this all bears looking into, and, of course, we need to catch this guy.

I'll bring it all up at the meeting on Monday night. You gonna be there?"

"Sure am chief, Suzanne too, if she's up to it."

The two men got up and made their way down the dark, narrow hall to the front door. "I look forward to seeing you both then. But, you know Steve, that was kind of a dumb thing you two did tonight. You might've been killed, but, I do appreciate the information. Good night now, and tell Suzanne, that Frances and I will be thinking of her. Tell her to take care now."

When Steve stepped outside, his watch said it was after 2 AM. Sunday already. There was nothing to do but return to his room at the Sandpiper Motel, and wait on Mondays' meeting.

Back in town, the man from the Murdoch Mansion had returned, and he lay on a skimpy mattress in his third floor hideaway, thinking back over the events of the night, his pulse racing, •and his head aching. He stared into the darkness like a frightened rabbit, until, at last, sleep overtook him.

Chapter Thirteen

It didn't take long for the chief's office to begin filling up. The public meeting was scheduled for eight o'clock, and by 7:15, it was practically standing room only, with just a few empty chairs. All the town's merchants were there, and some from the outlying areas in the county. Pykes County had an abundance of antique and novelty shops, and, it seemed, all were ably represented.

Suzanne came in at 7:30, escorted by Steve, and took a seat next to Edna Brown. The sisters always dressed alike, and tonight they were wearing identical flowered dresses, and carried big, straw handbags.

Clyde McMartin and Judy Wagner were sitting front and center, and Kevin McLaughlin stood in front of the chief's podium conversing with Steve. Homer Bradshaw from the dry dock was in animated conversation with Sam Myers, and Cassie Edelson, one of the Yacht Club waitresses was adjusting her hair in her mirror. Suzanne couldn't help notice that Cassie rotated the mirror around the room, in order to get a good look at everyone else who was there.

Mildred Jenkins and Buster came in, followed by Mildred's sister, Gladys, and, just as the chief was asking everyone to settle down, Lorraine scooted in, and took the last seat available, right next to one of the outlying antique dealers. She discreetly placed her business card in the man's hand, nodded, and turned her attention to Chief Morgan.

Raising his hands to get everyone's attention, Arthur Morgan looked weary, even before he started.

"Ladies and Gentlemen, thank you all for coming. Our friend Steve Thomas here has shared some new information with me this past weekend, and, I think it needs to be shared with all of you. Steve, how bout comin up here and tellin these folks about your adventure last Saturday night."

Glancing quickly at Suzanne, Steve took his place in front of the merchants.

"Friends, I know you have all experienced some form of petty theft or vandalism over these past few weeks, but, Chief Morgan and I think we know who is responsible."

That revelation seemed to electrify all, and murmurs rippled through the crowd.

"Seems this past Saturday, a friend and I noticed what appeared to be a dim light coming from inside the Murdoch Mansion.............."

Impatient as always, his face beet red, Sam Myers waved a hand at Steve, and interrupted him "Ah, cut to the quick Thomas. Tell us who the scoundrel is so we can have him arrested."

It was tall, lanky, Kevin McLaughlin who jumped to his feet, and quieted the crowd. When everyone had again settled down, he nodded for Steve to continue.

Sitting in the back, Suzanne looked stricken. Hoping the folks wouldn't become unruly, she was looking for an early night, so she could get back home and rest. Her head still throbbed from the fall she had taken Saturday night, but, she wanted to show support for the town's efforts to put a stop to the thievery. She smiled at Steve, and mentally encouraged him to continue.

"Folks, let Thomas here continue." It was Chief Morgan with his arms raised against the underlying hum of conversation in the room. "Please, Steve, go on."

"Well..............," before he could get another word out, the entire building was rocked by an explosion. The men couldn't get to the windows fast enough to see what was going on, and Steve and Kevin rushed outside just in time to see the Murdoch Mansion literally explode into flames. The house was fully engulfed in fire, as residents ran about the street. The Chief dispatched the fire department, which shared the municipal building with his police officers, and Sam Myers hurried down the street towards his own home, in the hopes of spraying water on it as a deterrent to the approaching fire. There was no way he was going to lose his house, even if the whole damn town burned down. Let them fight their fire, he thought, he was saving his own place.

Suzanne and the Brown sisters stood outside the police department, and watched in horror as the towns landmark burned. It was a roaring fire, with lots of smoke, and the chief had already called for backup from Baylors Point.

Edna Brown was trembling as she gripped Suzanne's arm.

"Oh dear, oh my goodness Suzanne, what in the world are we going to do? This is just awful, why, that place was the grandest you've ever seen. Oh the parties and dances, why, you just can't imagine."

"Yes, parties and dances," echoed Miss Harriette, as she stood there, next to her sister, both ladies shaking their heads in disbelief. "Just awful."

Suzanne didn't know where to go with the Browns, it was obvious no one was leaving the street. Everyone in town had come out to watch the fire department pour water on what was surely the loveliest house ever built. They couldn't all stand in the same spot. Signaling one of the other police officers to get some chairs for Edna and Harriette, Suzanne left them in the yard of the municipal building, and made her way through the crowd that was standing on the sidewalk watching the Murdoch Mansion and all its memories, burn to the ground.

The fire was so intense, the flowers in nearby flower boxes, and in the medians of the streets all wilted from the heat. Steve and Kevin, along with some of the other men, assisted the fire departments with the blaze. Sometime later in the evening, a worker from the yacht club brought pitchers of ice water and some pastries to the fire fighters. Spectators milled about, speaking in hushed tones, as they watched the fire slowly ebb away. Long after the flames were extinguished, the smoke continued, as the embers smoldered. Trees on the estate were blackened, and the lawn was virtually destroyed after fire vehicles, hose and men trampled on it all night.

Suzanne had been observing all evening, had lost track of the time, and, when she turned around to check on Miss Edna and Miss Harriette, they were gone. Good thing, she reasoned, they needed to be in bed, and not staying out here looking at a piece of town history go down the tubes.

It was close to midnight when Lorraine came to stand beside her. "So, what d'ya think Suze? What are we going to do with all this burned wood, and water soaked brick? Nice piece of property, I guess it could be developed."

Suzanne stared at her friend in disbelief. "Lorraine, I can't understand you sometimes. Why would you even consider putting some kind of development on this corner? They'll most likely tear it down and just make it a park of some kind. Put a plaque in probably, but this is Murdoch property, and I don't see how it can be anything else."

"Well, I reckon you're right. Say, Steve never got to finish his story, and the chief never had his meeting either! Now what?" Lorraine pulled her sweater closer around her shoulders. Her red hair gleamed in the moonlight. Too tall and thin by most standards, Suzanne still adored her friend. They had been best buddies since the third grade at Pykes

County School, and, in spite of Lorraine's insane ways, Suzanne Coldwell always was supportive of her, and they shared a mutual concern for the other's welfare.

"You chilly?" Suzanne rubbed Lorraine's arms. "Poor thing, you have no meat on your bones. Why don't you go on home, I'm going to stick around till they're finished, then maybe have some coffee with Steve."

Lorraine gazed fondly at her friend. Pushing tendrils, of hair out of her face, she nodded. "Not chilly, really, just kind of shivery. All that cold water spraying about, I think I just got too wet." The last sentence was said through a sneeze, as Lorraine slipped her arms into the sweater.

"Go on home, Rainey," Suzanne said. "I'll let you know any new developments." She watched as Lorraine disappeared into the night, waving to some of the other spectators as she went.

Finally, the fire hoses were pulled back into the trucks, the equipment stowed, once more, in their assigned spaces on the sides of the fire engines, and folks slowly began to drift away. Chief Morgan was deep in conversation with the fire chiefs from Beryl's Cove and Baylors Point, and, the firefighters were taking off their heavy coats and helmets. Several of them produced handkerchiefs with which to wipe their faces. Steve walked over to where Suzanne was standing, had been standing all evening, watching him. His clothes were wet and sooty, but they embraced for a long while. Pulling away, she gazed up into his tired face.

"C'mon, let's go home. I can make you some coffee, run you a bath, what do you say?"

Putting his arm around her shoulder, Steve waved to the others. "Coldwell, you don't know how nice that sounds. Maybe a nice, soft bed too, and someone to cuddle up with would be great!" The two of them set off down the street towards Eventide Lane, and Suzanne's cottage.

While Steve soaked all the soot and tiredness out of his body, Suzanne put the coffee pot on. The grandfather clock in the living room chimed the three o'clock hour. The fire had burned for hours, and then it was several more hours until all the embers were out. What lay on the ground now were piles of smoking wood, roof shingles, and hot bricks. Suzanne was bone tired, but not quite ready for sleep. Adrenalin had been pumping all evening, and she needed to decompress somewhat before sleep would overtake her.

She carried a tray with cups of coffee onto the side porch, and lit a table lamp, casting a soft glow in the room. She was sitting on the wicker settee, feet propped up, when Steve joined her. He had one of Suzanne's big, plush towels wrapped around his waist. Sitting on the sofa drinking their coffee, they listened to the crickets in the yard. A small breeze found its way in through the screens, and Suzanne just could not think of anything she would rather be doing, than sitting here with this man, whom she was beginning to care for deeply. They were jarred out of their reverie by the ringing of the phone. Giving Steve a quizzical look, and a shrug of her shoulders, she went to answer it. She returned to the porch with the portable phone and handed it to Steve.

"Chief Morgan wants to speak with you."

"Chief, what can I do for you?" Steve watched as Suzanne drank her coffee, and he listened to what the chief had to say. Nodding occasionally, and making few remarks, he thanked Morgan for calling, and hung up. He sat staring for the longest time, then he glanced up at Suzanne. "They found a body in the debris from the fire Suze. In the basement. When the fire department went back in to hose it down one more time, and check to make sure the blaze was completely out, they found a man in the rubble. Tall, heavy-set guy. Morgan thinks it was Lester Pruitt, the caretaker, and the same guy that found us snooping around. Said the body is being taken to Raleighs' medical examiner for an autopsy, but he seems to think this will close the case.

Of course, all the stuff that was stolen has been destroyed in the fire, so no one will get anything back, but this pretty much wraps it up, if the town can just figure out what to do with a burned out shell of an old house."

Suzanne was stunned, this was more than anyone had bargained for. What a tragic ending to what was once a magnificent home and estate. "I don't know what to say," she barely spoke. "Steve, you might have been hurt, or killed, and I don't think I could handle that." All the excitement of the weekend suddenly came to the surface, and she collapsed in Steve's arms, sobbing as if her heart would break. Sometime after 4 am they fell asleep in each other's arms.

Chapter Fourteen

It was several days later when the official autopsy report came back across the desk of Chief Morgan. He asked Alice to call all the shop owners and ask them to meet him in his office after closing time, for a brief meeting.

The meeting with the chief was scheduled for 7 PM, and it seemed like a repeat of the night the house burned. Everyone in town was there, all anxious to hear the final report.

Arthur Morgan came around his desk and looked at the crowd that had gathered. Clearing his throat, he waved the paper above his head to get attention.

"Folks," he began. "This here is the autopsy report on our dead body that was found in the embers of the Murdoch Mansion. Raleigh says that by comparing dental records, etc. they have made a positive identification of one, Lester James Pruitt. You all may recall that Eleanor Murdoch was a Pruitt, and Lester seems to be the son of a second cousin to her. Far as we know, there is no other kin, or surviving family members, so this pretty much shuts the door on our investigation. Let's wait for the dust to settle before we decide what we are going to do with this property. Any questions?"

Kevin McLaughlins hand shot up. "Why'd he do it chief?"

Morgan shook his head at the crowd. "I reckon that's something we'll never know Kevin, his reason died with him in the fire. Maybe he didn't like the town, maybe to pay us back for a long ago transgression, who knows? I'll get in touch with the attorney for the estate as soon as is feasible. In the meantime, thank you for coming, and I hope you have a good evening."

The chief returned to the business side of his desk and began shuffling papers as the merchants of Beryl's Cove filed out of his office.

Kevin stood with Steve and Suzanne outside the building, and watched as everyone went their own way. Lorraine had offered a lift to the Browns, everyone else appeared to be walking. As the crowd dispersed, he turned to look at Steve. Offering a pat on the shoulder to Suzanne, he said, "Well, maybe now we can all put our lives back together. You folks have a good night." Shaking hands with Steve, Kevin walked to his car parked at the curb.

Steve and Suzanne waved as he drove away, and walked arm and arm up the street towards her cottage. It was 7:30 at night, and a calm had settled over the town that evening. The smell of smoke was still heavy in the air, but peace and serenity had returned to the Cove. The only problem now was what to do with the burned out shell of the mansion that stood like a charred skeleton in the middle of the block.

Chapter Fifteen

Summer in Beryl's Cove brings a plethora of tourists. They love the location for charter boat fishing, they go antiquing, and they spend their days strolling the tree lined streets, shopping, and eating seafood in the local restaurants.

Tourist season was in full swing at the Cove, as Suzanne and the other residents kept busy in their respective businesses. Her antiques were selling well, so well in fact, that she had left Roger in charge while she made a quick buying trip to New York. It was all the two of them could do to keep the inventory moving, and sweep out the store every day.

Lorraine's summer rentals were full, and she had a few listings out in the county she was showing on a regular basis. Mark and Jean Roberts were so thrilled with their house, they were trying to get Lorraine in touch with friends of theirs who were looking for coastal property.

The Lucky Lady was out of drydock, and Steve was taking tourists out on it on a regular basis. He had not planned to run a charter service, but there didn't seem to be enough boats this season, so, he hired a first mate, and they were in business. Staying so busy at the dock all the time, left little opportunities for romancing Suzanne, but they did manage to grab a quick bite at the yacht club every so often. They still had not formalized their living arrangements, but, they were in agreement that as soon as they had the time, they would figure something out. Steve slept on board, and, after many a late night at the store, Suzanne literally poured herself into bed.

Edna and Harriette Brown were doing a booming business. The town council had contracted with them to replace all the median flowers around town that had wilted from the intensity of the fire at the Murdoch Mansion. They had had to send to Baylors Point for some blooms, but, on the whole, they were enjoying doing something for the town that they felt was so worthy.

The Murdoch Mansion stood like a shadowy scarecrow against the Carolina sky. A partial frame, and most of the basement remained as a skeletal reminder of better times. The grounds were beginning to replenish themselves, and nothing yet had been decided about clearing the land. Chief Morgan's attempts to locate the estate attorney were frustrating at best. Finally reaching him one day, he told the chief for the town to come up with a proposal for the land and get back to him. Arthur Morgan was stymied about any further developments in the case. His only concern at the moment was keeping order with the tourists, and making plans for the Rotary Clubs', hopefully, peaceful July 4th celebration.

It was a steamy June Saturday when Suzanne opened her shop for the visiting out of towners. Busying herself behind the counter, she failed to hear when MaeRuth Miller entered the store about 9:30. Looking up to see her, Suzanne came around the counter and hugged her longtime friend.

"My, aren't you a sight MaeRuth! Have you and Jack gotten settled in that new house yet? Gosh, it seems like an age since we've seen you around town." Leading her lawyer's wife over to the window seat, she motioned for her to sit. "Would you like something to drink, a coke, coffee?"

"Oh my no, Suzanne, but thanks anyway. I needed to come to town just to get reconnected with all our friends.

Look, I know this is short notice, but Jack and I were planning on having a little gathering tomorrow afternoon around four, just to kind of show off our new place, so to speak, and I was hoping you and Steve could make it. Do you think so?"

"Why, MaeRuth, we'd be delighted. Everybody has been so interested in that place you built, you couldn't keep us away. Do you like living out on the bluff?"

"More than you can imagine Suze," MaeRuth fairly gushed about her new home, to anyone who would inquire. "You don't need to bring a thing, just your sweet self and that handsome devil you've been seeing," She got up to leave, waving to Roger in the back of the store. Out on the street, she waved to several passersby as she got in her Lincoln and drove off.

The rest of the morning was busy, despite the heat, there seemed to be a lot of visitors in town, and the yacht basin was busy as always. Suzanne left at noon to meet Steve at the yacht club for lunch.

Slipping into the corner booth that had become their favorite, Steve gave her a peck on the cheek and squeezed her hand as he sat down next to her. Signaling the waiter to bring them iced tea, he nuzzled the back of her neck.

Suzanne laughed as she playfully pushed him away. "Darling, please, you know I don't like you playing in public. Besides, I have something to tell you. MaeRuth and Jack Miller have built that big house out on the bluff, and they're having a house warming tomorrow at four, and we've been invited. Is it ok that I have accepted for us?"

Steve was holding her hand, and caressing her arm as he spoke. "You know your beauty drives me insane woman? Where have you been all my life?"

Suzanne pulled her arm away as the waiter brought their tea, and took their order for roast beef sandwiches. "Steve please, is it ok?"

"Of course it's ok. Fine with me, anything you want to do. Who are these people again?"

"Jack is my attorney, he was my folks corporate attorney, and an old family friend. His wife MaeRuth is real sweet, and they built that huge house out on the bluff as you head towards Bradshaws Dry Dock, on the other side of the Harbor View townhouses."

"Oh yeah, I saw it when I went out there to see the chief the night we were attacked. Beautiful place. He have enough business in this town to build something like that?"

Suzanne put down her sandwich to wipe her mouth. "Well, he's just about the only game in town, although he does have some others in practice with him, they are really just part-time, coming in once or twice a month from their offices at Baylors Point or Pykes Bay. Jack handles everybody's business here, plus all the real estate closings, so, I guess he does pretty well. I think MaeRuth came into some money when her grandparents died or something. Why, does it matter?"

"No, of course not, just curious. Hey, I've got to tell you something too. I hate to do it Suze, but I need to go to Norfolk for a couple of weeks. I need to meet with M.J., check on my stock, do some work around the shop, that sort of thing. Plus, I have a meeting with some government people up there. I'll be back as soon as I can." He kissed her hand, as he so gallantly did so often. "I'll miss you terribly. Promise me you'll miss me too?"

"Oh Steve, of course I will. You do what you have to, I'll be right here. I um, just hate that you can't take part in the 4th of July boat regatta. Uh, I thought you were entering the Lucky Lady in that."

"Yeah, well, this trip really needs to be made, and the sooner the better. There will be other regattas. Believe me Suze, I wouldn't go if it wasn't absolutely necessary. My life is here now, with you. How bout we leave it at that, and I'll pick you up tomorrow at 3:45 or so. Can we walk to the Miller place, or take the car?"

Suzanne was taken aback at Steve's sudden aloofness. She was trying to digest what he had said, but she honestly didn't know why he had to go now, during the height of the summer season. Those old feelings of doubt were creeping back in. She gazed into the face of the man she had come to care so much for, but he was busy with his sandwich. He had not even left yet, and, already she missed him.

"When are you going?" she asked him.

"Monday, we'll get this party over with, and, then, I can leave." He put his napkin down on the table, took another sip of his tea before kissing Suzanne. He gave her a quizzical look as he pulled some money out of his billfold for the lunch.

"What?"

"Oh nothing, I was just thinking it was too hot to walk out there, we'd better drive."

Signaling the waiter again, Steve got up and held out his hand for her. "Great, let's go, I really need to get my stuff together, and check out the Lady before I sail. I'll see you tomorrow."

They walked on the boardwalk back to the antique store, where Steve left her to return to the marina. Suzanne busied herself with customers all afternoon until well past closing time.

Arriving home at 7, she phoned Lorraine and asked if she was up for carry out pizza. Delighted that her friend was available to her, Lorraine hurried down the street to the Coldwell cottage, where she walked in and found her in tears on the living room sofa.

"Hey, what's up? Suze, what is it?"

"Oh Raine, I'm being so silly, it's just that Steve is leaving for "two weeks, and I'm being a big baby about the whole thing. My God, sometimes I can't believe I'm fifty years old!"

Settling on the sofa, with her feet on Suzanne's coffee table, Lorraine helped herself to a slice of pizza.

"Honey, you don't have to be a certain age to be too old to cry over a man. What I want to know is, why he hasn't asked you to marry him, or at least moved in with you. Is he ..." Lorraine gestured in circles with her hand, "You know, all right?"

Suzanne wiped her eyes, and blew her nose, and reached for the pizza. "Don't be stupid, Rainey, of course he's as all right as it's possible to be. I'm just being silly, and we haven't even discussed marriage. We were going to move in together, but things keep happening, like our attack, the fire, you know, we just haven't gotten around to it. Maybe after all the rush of the summer season we can do it. I just don't understand his going now, with the boat regatta and all coming up. It just seems so sudden, it's like he can't wait to get out of town!"

Sighing, they ate in silence, and decided to make it an early night, talking the next afternoon at the Millers' party.

Chapter Sixteen

Sunday was a beautiful day, sunny and warm. The restaurants were bustling, and most of the shop owners opened for half a day anyway, during the season. After early church service, Suzanne dashed over to the shop where Roger told her he had sold a few things, the yellow antique Victorian sofa among them. He had sold it over the phone to a customer in Virginia, he said.

After lunch, Suzanne put out her closed sign and walked the two blocks to her house. Perspiring in the heat, she decided to shower before she changed for the Millers.

Choosing a lightweight polished cotton sundress, she was putting on some low heeled espadrilles when Steve arrived with a bouquet of Black Eyed Susan's for her.

"Ooh, they are lovely, and you are wonderful." Kissing him tenderly, she leaned into his chest with a sigh. "You are so good for me darling, I just feel all warm and fuzzy when we're together."

Encircling her with his arms, Steve kissed the top of her head." That's good, me too. Roger had told me how much you love Black Eyed Susans, and the Browns had a big batch of them to come in, so I couldn't resist. As nice as this is, we'd better be going, don't you think?" He held her at arm's length and gave her an approving look. "You're gorgeous, now, put those in water, and let's go." He swatted her lightly on the rear as she turned to take the flowers into the kitchen for a vase.

Pulling up in the Millers' circular drive, Suzanne saw that judging by the number of early arrivals, this was going to be a big party. As they got out of her car, she noticed Clyde McMartins' car coming around the curve towards the house. Judy Wagner was in the front seat with him. She made a mental note to ask Lorraine about that liaison, Clyde was easily fifteen years older than Judy, and up until the night of the fire, no one had seen them together, now they went everywhere as a couple.

MaeRuth was in a flowered MuuMuu, with an Hibiscus in her hair when she answered the door. She ushered them into the sunken great room and took their drink order. Jack Miller approached them, drink in hand, and kissed Suzanne's cheek while he shook hands with Steve. "My dear, I am so glad you could make it. We're all set up on the patio, why don't we go out there? We are having an Hawaiian Luau tonight, MaeRuth's idea, I'm afraid. Steve, good to see you. C'mon, the view is spectacular out here."

Arthur and Frances Morgan were in rattan lounge chairs; Sam Myers stood by the bar, and Mark and Jean Roberts were engaged in animated conversation with Kevin McLaughlin. Suzanne and Steve were breathless of the view of the ocean, and the relaxed atmosphere of the gathering did much to calm her nerves. She was determined to not think about Steve's leaving tonight, she was simply going to enjoy the party.

The revelers were in full swing, and having a grand time. MaeRuth periodically led small groups through her new home, and Steve and Suzanne enjoyed talking in small groups with their friends and neighbors. From the corner of her eye, she saw Lorraine approaching. Taking a sip of her wine, she patted the sofa next to her for her friend. Plopping down, rather indelicately, Suzanne thought, Lorraine put her plate of food in her lap, and leaned towards her best friend.

"Do you see that hussy with Clyde McMartin? She has some nerve, a young whip like that taking old Clyde out of circulation and away from us more seasoned women."

"Judy? Well, I wouldn't exactly call her a hussy Raine. What's wrong with her, and what's wrong with you for worrying about it?" Looking at her friend wide-eyed, she put down her drink and faced Lorraine. "Don't tell me you have the hots for him! My God, Raine, he couldn't handle you!"

"Don't be crude girlfriend, it's just that she should stick to guys her own age, like some high school kid." Lorraine sipped her drink and waved to someone across the room.

Suzanne laughed as she smiled up at Steve, who was deep in conversation with Mark Roberts. "Raine, you are a piece of work. I know you were married once to Judy's brother, but, for petes sake, let it go. She's ok, just a little young. Maybe Clyde likes them that way. "Wasn't one of your exes younger than you?"

"Oh pooh," Lorraine fairly spat, "by six months, big deal! Besides, it's different with those two. At least I was old enough to know better." Turning to look at Suzanne she continued, "so, are you going to the 4th of July festivities even though Honey Bun there won't be in town?" She nodded at Steve, but continued to look into the face of her dear friend.

"Of course, although I'll miss seeing him in the boat regatta. Raine, excuse me, I think I need to speak to Jean Roberts. You behave now." Suzanne left her friend with a pat on her shoulder, and went to where Steve was talking with Mark Roberts. Jean was standing silently by her husband when Suzanne approached.

"Jean, how are you?" she asked.

Jean Roberts was a slender woman, always fashionably dressed, but, she seemed to Suzanne, a little vacuous. She never had much to say to folks, but she seemed genuinely happy to see Suzanne.

"Oh, hey, yes I'm fine. Isn't this a perfectly lovely home? So comfortable and beautifully furnished, and boy, what a view!"

The two women gazed out at the ocean from the wraparound windows of the Millers' sun porch. The ocean was beautiful, and rather tranquil for this time of year. A month into hurricane season, and so far, the coast of North Carolina has been spared any storm. Warm and muggy days, Suzanne silently prayed for an inactive hurricane season. The fire that had destroyed the Murdoch Mansion had disrupted the tourist season quite enough, they didn't need a major storm to rip into town and upset it even further.

It was close to 8:00, and the Millers' open house had been going on since 4. As the day wore on, the party goers began to leave. Town folks, and virtually all the shop owners has been invited, and MaeRuth was a gracious hostess. Born into the South of the "old school" manners, she had been trained properly in the art of gracious hostessing, and everyone had felt most welcome.

Explaining that he had to get an early start in the morning, Steve dropped Suzanne at home, and staying only an hour to talk, he left, and walked towards the marina where the Lucky Lady was moored.

It was 11:00, and Suzanne was still sitting in her darkened bedroom, staring out at the ocean two blocks away, and, turning around to look out another window, she saw the ghostly outline of the Murdoch house standing in the moonlight.

Such a beautiful, stately home, and now it was gone. The Murdochs would turn over in their grave, she thought, if they could see the burned out shell it had become.

She got into bed and fell asleep wondering if things would ever be back to normal in Beryl's Cove again. The town landmark was gone, and nobody seemed overly concerned with it. There had to be something they could do with the property, but where to start, and who to do it? She was determined to look into it in the morning, or at least as soon after the 4th celebration that she could.

Steve would be gone two weeks, he said, maybe more. Plenty of time she thought to do some research, and find out what the town could do with the Murdoch property. In her mind's eye, she still saw a park there, but as sleep overtook her, all she could think about was how much she would miss him.

Chapter Seventeen

July 4th arrived hot and steamy in North Carolina. It fell in the middle of the week, but the Cove was crowded with visitors, and the harbor was abloom with sails of every shape and size, as the regatta got under way. The boardwalk that ran in front of the yacht club was lined with chairs and umbrella tables, and one end of the walk held a table loaded with hot dogs, hamburgers and soft drinks. All the wait staff from the yacht club had been working since early morning to insure that nobody went hungry or thirsty. There was plenty for all, as most of the locals sat at tables eating and watching the parade of boats. Lorraine and Suzanne wore matching straw hats with red, white, and blue ribbons; Arthur and Frances Morgan were in tennis whites hoping for a game after lunch, and the Brown sisters sat fanning themselves on chairs close to the food. Kevin McLaughlin and his family were manning the ticket booth in the middle of town. Mildred and Buster Jenkins had left Gladys in charge of the Seabreeze Inn, and had walked over to join in the day's festivities. Slathered in sunscreen Mildred was very animated as she gossiped with anyone within ear shot.

The townspeople were everywhere, some down on the beach, where the sand was crowded with families, and, it seemed every dog in Pykes County. One in particular kept up a constant yapping at the boats as they glided by. Off by himself, sitting in a deck chair, and scowling at the kids building sand castles, Sam Myers sat in a straw hat, dungarees, and Hawaiian shirt, a big cigar stuck in his mouth. He seemed particularly interested in one of the sailboats out on the water.

"Now, what do you s'pose has got him so wound up and looking so interested" Frances Morgan seemed to be speaking more to herself than anyone else. Looking over at her, her husband smiled. "Sam Myers is interested only in himself, my dear, but I also know he bet a bundle on that lead boat, the one with the blue stripe on her sail."

Overhearing the conversation, Lorraine turned towards Morgan. "Betting on our regatta? Isn't there a law against that chief? Why that's positively sinful! It takes all the fun out of it."

Arthur Morgan wiped his brow with his hand, adjusted his sunglasses, and, putting them back on, he looked over the top of them at Lorraine.

"Yes, Lorraine, it's against the law, but, as I see it, it's just a friendly wager between him and Claude. I don't think it's anything more than two old friends waging a small amount on the football games. Besides, it's only something. I heard, can't prove anything, and, I'm not wanting to either. Now don't worry your pretty little head over it." Turning back to face the water, he muttered something about two more years under his breath. Frances smiled and winked at Lorraine. Suzanne got up and wandered over to the food table. She was going to get hamburgers and drinks for her and Rainey, when Edna Brown tugged at her sleeve. "Suzanne, you look positively radiant, could it be that new man in your life?" She smiled and nodded to her sister Harriette.

"Yes, new man," Harriette echoed.

Patting the old woman on the hand, Suzanne gave her a bright smile, and winked at her twin sister. "Why Miss Edna, I do believe we need to find a nice young set of twins for the two of you. Some tall, dark, handsome strangers who love flowers, and can keep up with you both."

The sisters giggled in tandem and increased their level of fanning. It was Edna who added, "Ooh Suzanne, do you think you could find us a couple of fellas?"

Nodding in agreement, Harriette added "fellas", causing Suzanne to laugh at the darling eccentrics.

Layering mustard and ketchup over the hamburgers, she grabbed two cokes, and a handful of chips before she waved to the Browns and went back to rejoin Lorraine.

As the day wore on, so did the sun, forcing the Brown sisters and some of the others to retreat to the cooled comfort of the yacht club.

The boat Sam Myers had been so interested in did indeed come in first, causing much cheering and glad handing among the men who had joined him on the beach to watch.

As dusk approached, beach goers, tourists, and locals staked out a spot on the sand to watch the fireworks. Someone had tuned a radio to patriotic music, and even the children seemed to settle down for the show.

The fireworks were spectacular, and around midnight, the crowds began to disperse. Mildred and Buster headed for the Inn, and a big crowd seemed headed for the Dry Dock Cocktail lounge on the other end of Ocean Park Drive.

Walking towards Eventide Lane, Lorraine and Suzanne watched the revelers heading up the street. "Want to go?" Lorraine asked.

Suzanne stopped where she was and gazed skyward at the beautiful Carolina moon. Every time she saw it, she knew why songs were written about the Carolina moon, as it was like no other. "No, I don't guess. I think I'll call it a night. You go, if you want Raine, don't stay behind on my account."

Lorraine kept her eyes on the twenty or so headed up the street. "You sure you don't mind Suze? I think I will, for a little while anyway. Maybe........ I'll see you tomorrow." With that, Lorraine was gone, and Suzanne turned down the Lane and headed home. Taking off her hat, she carried it in her hand as she mounted the steps of her cottage.

Once inside, she turned the hall light on, but instead of going upstairs to bed, she went out onto the sunporch. There she sat down on her chaise and looked out the screen to the sky. Where, she wondered, was Steve on this night, and what was he doing? Was he thinking of her, or had he just made a hasty retreat back to Norfolk?

Maybe, she thought, Lorraine was right. Maybe she should be more aggressive and pin him down with something definite. Marriage? She hadn't really thought much about it, she had always been too busy with her career to contemplate marriage. Besides, she reasoned, there just wasn't anybody who could get her in the marrying mood. Until Steve, that is. He was everything she had ever looked for in a man; he was sweet, considerate of her, intelligent, handsome. "Yes," she said aloud, "and set in his ways, exasperating, and then there's that Elvis thing." She had never met anyone who was such a fan of a celebrity as to open up a shop for just that persons memorabilia. She wondered if that would be considered childish. She wondered if she were being childish.

Talking out loud to herself, she added, "Suzanne, old girl, you're just going to have to get used to him. I was looking for someone when he walked into my life, and I can look for someone again."

Right, her subconscious told her, sure you can. Tired of arguing with herself, she left the porch and went upstairs to bed. As she lay there in the darkness, she could hear fireworks off in the distance. Kids, probably, she thought, as she drifted off to sleep.

Chapter Eighteen

It had been almost three weeks since Steve had gone to Norfolk. Suzanne had received intermittent phone calls from him declaring how busy he was, but, he assured her, he would return within the month. In the meantime, he was sending M.J. with some plans for her to look at.

What kind of plans, she wanted to know. He didn't say, just that it would set Beryl's Cove on its ear, and that M.J. would be there soon.

One Thursday afternoon, business in the Cove had slowed enough for Suzanne to work on inventory and pricing in the back of the store. She left Roger in front to wait on the few customers that were coming in that week. Schools always began in August in the Carolinas, so many vacationers headed home the latter part of July to prepare for it. Some of Lorraine's summer tenants had already packed up and left.

Suzanne, coke in hand, and dust cloth in the other, was in the storeroom this particular afternoon when Roger entered the back room.

"Whoa, get a load of the hot babe in the front! Man, Suze, you ain't never seen anything like this, c'mon, have a look." Gently, he led her over to the curtain that separated the back area from the showroom. Suzanne peeked out to see a stunning blonde, in a black pantsuit and stiletto heels. She was tanned to a golden bronze, wore too much makeup, and had her hair piled up with several tendrils hanging around her heart shaped face.

"Hmph, she probably wants an imitation bronze something or other. You're welcome to her Roger, I have work to do." As she returned to her pricing, Roger stopped her.

"Not so fast, old girl, she's asking for you."

"Me?" Suzanne raised an eyebrow as she stole another peek at the woman. "I don't know anyone looks like that, and what's with this 'old girl' business?" Laughing, she entered the store front where the woman was standing. Putting her dust cloth down, she extended her hand to her.

"Hi, I'm Suzanne Coldwell, the owner, can I help you?"

Flashing a dazzling smile that Suzanne felt sure was phony, the woman shook her hand. "Sure can, I'm M.J., M.J. Follett."

It was seconds before Suzanne remembered to close her mouth. Suddenly, she felt old and slovenly. Before she could recover, M.J. spoke again.

"You know, Steve's friend. He did tell you I was coming didn't he?"

"Um, why yes, of course, it's just that, uh, well," Suzanne gave a meek little laugh. "You're not, um, exactly what I had in mind. He never said you were a woman. How long have you been this way?" Why was she being so awkward, she wondered, she felt like a school girl.

M.J. was used to this kind of thing, she got it all the time. Try as she could to be just one of the girls, she knew that as long as she looked like she did, women would be uncomfortable around her. She felt sorry for Suzanne, who was, after all, a beautiful woman in her own right. Maybe her height was intimidating her.

Laughing, M.J. removed her shoes and looked into Suzanne's chocolate brown eyes. "If you mean how long have I been a woman, all my life, thank you. Look," She said, rubbing her feet. "These things really kill me, mind if I sit down?" She walked over to the rocking chair in front of the window and sat, dangling her shoes off the tip of her index finger. She motioned for Suzanne to sit in the other chair. "Steve never tells anyone I'm a woman, I don't think he thinks of me in quite that way. We've been partners for many years, you know. I think he just considers me a business associate.

Smiling, barely, Suzanne couldn't imagine any man not thinking of M.J. as a woman. She was at a loss, and had no idea of what to say next. Clearing her throat, she looked around the shop before saying anything at all.

"Tell me.......M.J., uh, what brings you here? Not that I'm not delighted to meet you, Steve really thinks you're great." Everything she said was turning out to be so inane, she just wanted the floor to open up and swallow her. This woman was drop dead gorgeous, and she was working with Steve, and, she realized, she didn't have a chance with him as long as M.J. Follett was around. She wanted to die on the spot.

M.J. rocked gently in the chair, eyeing Suzanne. She really felt sympathy for the charming Miss Coldwell. "Look, Suzanne, let's get one thing out of the way right now, I am not after Steve. I have a boy friend, thank you very much, I just work with him, that's all. Most of the time, I work without him, running his business. I have a brain, you know."

Taken aback by M.J.'s bluntness, she knew the woman was probably seeing right through her, and here she was being a dummy and forgetting her manners. Mama would turn in her grave, she thought to herself. "I....I'm sorry, M.J., was I that transparent? You must be hot and tired, do you want to walk down to the yacht club for a sandwich and cold drink or maybe the pub-like atmosphere of the Dry Dock would suit you better, or of course, we could go to the pizza place out on the highway, oh, you know what? There is this neat tearoom over in Baylors Point............"

M.J. stared at Suzanne in disbelief, "please lady, you're babbling."

Blushing, Suzanne stopped. "I am, aren't I? I'm sorry M.J. What would you like to do?"

M.J. bent over to put her shoes back on, and, as she was redoing the straps, she gazed up at Suzanne. "First things first. I've been here what, 5 minutes" I've left the car running because Elvis is in there, and I want to keep him cool. Steve thought it was time he brought him here to Beryl's Cove. Steve wants Elvis with him, and he thought maybe you'd keep him for a few days till he gets back." Straightening up, she began gathering her handbag, and stood up. "So, how about it, should we go get him?"

"Elvis?"

M.J. was out the door and opening the door of her Wagoneer before Suzanne could gather her thoughts. Rushing after her, she stood back as M.J. brought forth from a pet carrier, a small, black and white cat, with the greenest eyes Suzanne has ever seen. Holding him out to her, M.J. said, "Suzanne, meet Elvis, Steve's cat."

The women both burst into peals of laughter as Suzanne took the cat and cuddled him. Elvis emitted a loud purr and nuzzled her neck.

"Oh, he's so adorable" How old is he?"

M.J. was climbing behind the wheel, motioning for Suzanne to get in the passenger side. "He's just three. Steve got him as a stray, and I've had him in Norfolk these past few months, mainly because Steve didn't want to put him on a boat, but, I think Elvis belongs with his dad. Now, where to, how bout we take ole El there to your house and get him situated, then, we'll go get us a bite to eat, and we'll talk. That ok?"

Dropping the cat and all his equipment off at the cottage, Suzanne was already in love with him, and hated to leave him to go anywhere, but, she and M.J. returned to the store to tell Roger to lock up, then they headed for the Dry Dock, and a quiet table in the corner.

Ordering beers and sandwiches, Suzanne marveled at M.J., and her strong personality, and her obvious obliviousness to the ogling men around her. She really did have a brain, and Suzanne was beginning to warm up to her.

Putting her napkin on her plate, M.J. leaned back in her chair and eyed the woman sitting across the table from her. "Well, I suppose you want to know where I fit in, and how I know Steve, and, more importantly, what I'm doing here, right?"

Suzanne nodded.

M.J. began after motioning for another beer from the bar tender. "It's like this, my older brother Pete knew Steve from the Navy. When they got out, I was still in college, so he and Pete decided to do this Elvis thing together, but neither one of them wanted to run it. Steve would rather be out and about buying, schmoozing, that sort of thing, and Pete, well, Pete's just a big hulk of a guy who would rather go fishing and hunting than running a business. Anyway, after I got my degree, we all put our heads together and opened the Elvis shop. We pooled our money, and with my brains, it's really been a going concern, but I handle the business end of it. Steve does most of the buying, and Pete, well, he finds investors, or scouts out estate sales, that sort of thing. Like I said, I'm not after Steve, you pretty much have him hog tied anyway." She paused to sip at her beer, and Suzanne was embarrassed to find herself once again blushing.

After a brief pause, M.J. continued. "The reason I'm here is because I am an expert in restoring old properties; historical restoration, with a minor in business was my course of study at William and Mary. Now, Steve has some ideas about restoring this Murdoch Mansion of yours, and he already had put into motion some plans for funding. What he needs from me is an opinion as to whether or not this place is worth the effort, and what exactly it means to the town. Has he spoken to you about any of this?"

"No, and quite frankly, I'm surprised. The house was pretty much destroyed in the fire, there's nothing left but a shell, although it was, at one time a lovely place. All the local girls had their debutante luncheons and such there. Then, of course, there were the tea dances. Really a beautiful time, the 50's. The house was elegant, and Mrs. Murdoch had a full staff to keep it that way. Oh M.J., do you really think it can be brought back?" Suzanne was becoming excited by the prospect of a once again elegant Murdoch Mansion.

"Well, that's what I want to find out. I need to speak with the so called powers that be, I need to see the ruins, if you will, and, I need to get myself a room somewhere while I'm here. By the way, Steve's in the shop in Norfolk, he'll return when I get back to relieve him, so, don't worry about him." She began gathering up her bag, and reached for the bill, but Suzanne quickly grabbed it, and shook her head.

"Not on your life, this is my treat. Forget about the room as well, you can stay with me, and in the morning, we'll go see Chief Morgan, and what's left of the house."

Chapter Nineteen

It was well past midnight, but neither Suzanne nor M.J. wanted to call it a night. With Elvis curled in her lap, purring contentedly, M.J. regaled her hostess with stories of Steve and her brother Pete. Suzanne had learned so much about him from her, she was reluctant to let her leave the room. It was comforting to learn from M.J. that Steve really did love her, mysterious though he may be. He had spent so many years in the Navy, living a rather solitary life, he was just accustomed to taking charge, making decisions, and going forward with them.

Replenishing their wine, Suzanne returned to the sofa and tucked her legs under her.

"M.J.," she began. "Uh, Steve came across as rather irresponsible when I first met him, I'm just having a really difficult time reconciling this new, improved version of Steve Thomas that you're presenting me with."

Stroking Elvis, and eliciting a louder purring from the cat, she raised an eyebrow as she stared blankly at Suzanne. "OH? How so, to me he's always been such an organized, methodical person. A lot of fun though, I can tell you. Steve loves a good joke or story, and boy can he pull a prank. Why, when he and Pete get together, it's downright raucous at times!"

Suzanne smiled, and reached for Elvis' ear. Petting behind the animal's ear, she broadened her smile as the cat stretched, yawned, and turned around on M.J.'s lap before falling back asleep.

"Well, for Instance, he doesn't have a car. Everywhere we go, we take mine, not that I really am concerned about it, you understand, it's just that, well, you'd think that once in a while he would want a car to drive somewhere." Motioning with her hand in a half wave, she said, "Oh forget about it. It doesn't matter, really it doesn't. Does he have any money?" she finally blurted.

Throwing her head back and laughing, M.J. woke Elvis, who jumped down and ran from the room. "My dear, Steve is loaded! All those years he and Pete served in the Navy together, all they ever did was play cards. They got pretty good at it, so, an occasional poker game is the only time they ever exchanged any money. Really, Steve is a good business man, and he saved a good bit of his pay, and, when he gambled in a game, he won. Now look honey, don't you go thinking Steve's got a problem, because he doesn't, but he likes a sure thing, why, we all do. I'm just saying, he doesn't take chances needlessly, but a sure thing, and boy, he's right there. Take his horse, for example. He owns part of a racehorse in Kentucky, and the blame thing can run like the wind. Set a new track record at Riverside Park, I'll have you know. Steve and Pete have gotten four times their money back on that horse, but you don't see him at the betting window for any other nag. See what I'm saying?"

Rising, M.J. stretched, took her wine glass over to the bar where she set it down, and faced Suzanne. "Girlfriend, I don't know about you, but I'm bushed. Let's say we call it a night, and meet in the morning to tackle our Chief Morgan. What do you say?"

"Of course, I am sorry, you must be exhausted after your drive from Norfolk. C'mon, we'll get up and start the day fresh tomorrow. Will you be all right down here by yourself? This is just a small cottage, actually, I'm thinking of knocking the wall out between the two guestrooms, and making one big room down here. Hey, give me a holler if you need anything, Ok, and there are more towels in that hall closet there if you need them."

M.J. was asleep in minutes, Elvis curled in a ball at her feet. Suzanne checked her e mail before going to bed, found a message from Steve, and took ten minutes to answer him, then, she, too was out like a light.

After a big breakfast, and a pot of strong coffee, the two women set out for Chief Morgan's office about 8:30. Alice, his secretary of long standing, showed them into his office almost immediately, where he rose at the sight of M.J. Nodding to Suzanne, he came around the desk and offered M.J. a chair. Returning to his chair, he leaned back and folded his hands, chapel fashion, across his stomach and gave the ladies his brightest smile.

"Now then, to what do I owe this pleasure, and how may I help you girls?"

Suzanne moved a little closer to the desk and looked back at the chief, who, it seemed, had eyes only for the engaging Miss Follett. "Chief," she began, "M.J. Follett here is representing Steve Thomas in a restoration project, hopefully anyway, of the Murdoch Mansion. What we need from you is to know if there might be any hindering legalities, or obstacles in the way of this project. Do we need to get written permission from anyone, in other words?"

Clearing his throat, and sitting up a little straighter, Arthur Morgan looked at the two attractive women facing him. He couldn't remember a time when so much beauty had been in his office at one time. It was enough to set a man to heating up some, right here at his desk. "Why no'm Miz Coldwell. You know, the estate attorney, what's his name, I. ... uh, can't think of his name offhand, but no, I don't expect there are any. Tell you what, you ladies go ahead and look over the place, and I'll look up that fellas name and give him a ring. He did say for us to come up with something for the property and get back to him. I swear, I've just been so busy, and I can't honestly think of anything to do with that old house cept tear down what remains of it. Now, if you two go around there, you be careful, those timbers that are left are half burned, and I don't know how good or sturdy any of the remains are. We've still got the yellow fire department tape around the whole shebang. Hey, maybe I should send one of my officers with you, what do you think, Suzanne?"

He ushered them out of the room as he spoke, and, after having been assured they would not go near the actual house, but just walk the grounds, he let them go, watching M.J. as they walked down the street to the Murdoch place.

As they approached the house from the east side, the women couldn't help laughing. They had to stop and lean against a tree and catch their breath, they were laughing so hard.

"Oh my God, is that man for real?" M.J. squeezed her sides as she tried to control herself. "Why, he is almost a caricature! How on earth do you Cove people put up with him?"

Running her hand through her auburn hair, Suzanne was still grinning broadly, "Oh, he's harmless really, just trying to serve out his last two years and get retired. He does very little really, we have a town council that does most of the work around here, but someone has to write the parking tickets. He makes a good visible image anyway. You ok now?"

Shaking her head, M.J. nodded in the direction of the side yard, and motioning for Suzanne, they took off in the direction of what was left of the house.

They walked around the Murdoch property several times, M.J. making notes, and fashioning drawings, asking questions, and looking.

Finally, they found a couple of tree stumps and perched half on and half off of them.

"You know," M.J. began, "this may not be as difficult as it seems, Suzanne. Look here, see where I drew what we call the basic footprint of the house? Well, it's still here."

"What does that mean?" Suzanne wanted to know.

"Look here," M.J. put her drawings in front of Suzanne. "You can see from the foundation that almost a complete outline of the house remains, and, it is from that outline that we will make a new blueprint. Look over there, at those tall timbers still standing by the chimney, that gives us an idea of how high the ceilings are. We really have a lot more to work with here than I originally thought. I can't wait to get back to Norfolk and start my research on this place, and get a set of blueprints for Steve. He's really the one spear heading this thing. Oh Suzanne, I'm so excited, he has such wonderful plans for this place, and, they include yourself I might add. Girl, you are going to be so pleased."

M.J. gathered her sketches, and together, the women walked back to Suzanne's cottage. Once inside, M.J. began packing her bag, after insisting that she had to get back to Norfolk and start to work.

"It's not the easiest drive, you know," she said over Suzanne's protestations. "The coastal highway is only two lanes, and you must know the traffic coming into Norfolk is a real bitch. Thanks, girlfriend for the hospitality, and I really appreciate your taking Elvis from me. I've only had him with me for six months, but I'm sure he misses Steve. He's kind of a nice cat anyway. "

Suzanne hugged her, and walked with her to the jeep. "Will you be coming back again? I've heard Steve talk so much about you, and, now that I've met you, he's absolutely right!"

Throwing her bag into the back seat, M.J. climbed behind the wheel. "Well, I guess this is it. I really love this town, and yes, you'll probably see me again, but, I know Steve is anxious to get back, so let me go. Take care of Elvis"

"One more thing," Suzanne leaned into the car through the window, and smiled at M.J.

"Yes?"

"What does the M.J. stand for?" She stood back as M.J. started to back up.

"Mary Jane!" She hollered and waved at the same time as she headed towards Ocean Park Drive and highway seventeen, and Norfolk.

Chapter Twenty

Suzanne busied herself in the shop the rest of that day, working late, she fell into bed close to midnight, Elvis laying across her feet and purring contentedly.

Eating a late breakfast the next day, she fed the cat, cleaned the litter box, and walked to the shop. She had not been there 20 minutes, when Edna and Harriette Brown walked over from next door. As usual, Edna did most of the talking.

"Oh, Suzanne," the old woman fairly gushed, and, by the looks of their flushed faces, they were certainly excited about something. "We heard about the restoration plans, this is the most exciting thing that's happened in the cove in years!"

"In years," echoed Harriette.

Edna sat down in the rocking chair and began a slow rock, while Harriette perched on the window seat, one leg dangling over the edge. "Why my dear, do you remember the glorious parties and soirees that house was privy to, and remember when old Mr. Murdoch, now, I'm talking about the grandfather here, remember when young Clarence brought home Eleanor Pruitt? Why, he liked to have thrown a kitten fit."

"Yes, he was in a fit, real good fit," Harriette nodded as she spoke.

Edna stopped rocking and looked up into Suzanne's eyes. "Why, old man Murdoch thought Eleanor to be from the wrong side, so to speak, but Eleanor, she fooled everybody. Sister, don't you remember that tea dance she gave right after the second war, and she wanted to pair up all the returning soldiers with the local Cove girls, that's when we had more permanent residents here than we have now. Remember that sister?"

Harriette was sitting so that she could swing one foot back and forth, and she nodded the entire time her twin was speaking. "Oh my yes, tea dance. That's the best time sister and I ever had. Oh Edna, if we could only have that house back where it was, my, my, that would be something."

Suzanne so enjoyed the Brown twins, and, with a little encouragement, they stayed a while longer reminiscing and even weeping a little over the glory that had been the Murdoch Mansion.

"Well," Edna got up from the rocker and motioned for Harriette to join her, "we've prattled on enough my dear, time to get to work. Harriette, we must go and let Suzanne get back to her store. This has been so nice dear one, but Sister and I must be going. Come Harriette."

It was late afternoon when a summer squall kicked up some wind and dumped sheet after sheet of rain. Water ran down the middle of the streets, and the wind upended the trash cans, and blew the geraniums at the door of the antique store into the street. When the rain stopped, and the sun came out again around five, Suzanne went out to sweep away the debris, and set about righting the flower pots that sat in front of all the stores on Seabreeze Avenue. She looked up just in time to see Steve Thomas walking briskly down the street towards the Dry Dock. He turned to smile and wave at her, and, pointing to his watch, he kept moving. She was so delighted to see him, she ran to the back room to smooth her hair and apply fresh lipstick, knowing he would stop on the way back from wherever he was headed.

Closing time came and went, and Steve had not returned. Suzanne told Roger to go on home, and she locked up, put the closed sign on her door, and walked home, where she set about preparing dinner for two, knowing Steve would be there any minute to share it with her. Splurging, she even picked some flowers from the yard for a vase she would put on the dinner table. She was so glad to see him, she could hardly contain herself as she waited dinner for him.

At 11:00, she blew out the candles, and ate her dinner, alone. Angry beyond words, she didn't know whether to cry or throw something. How, she wondered, could M.J. consider him so responsible when he behaved this way towards her. She wanted to kill him. Instead, she picked up Elvis and stroked the cat's fur behind his ears. Elvis started an appreciative purring, and nudged her chin while she carried him upstairs to bed.

After watching the late news with Steve's cat, she turned out the light, rolled over, and tried to sleep, but she was so distraught, it would be many hours before sleep would come.

In the meantime, Steve was talking with Sam Myers and Jack Miller in the parking lot of the Dry Dock. He had lost all track of the time, when, looking at his watch, he realized it was after 2 A.M. Begging off, he sprinted down Ocean Park Drive to Eventide Lane, where he turned and headed for Suzanne's cottage.

He found the cottage dark when he got here. He walked up to the door and tried to peer in the tiny, moon-shaped window, but saw nothing. Jumping down to the ground, he went around to the back, and looked up at Suzanne's windows, but they, too were dark. Searching the ground, he found a small pebble and tossed it up towards the second story. It barely touched the window. He retrieved another and tossed it upwards, where it hit the second story window with a ping before falling at his feet. Getting no response, he thrust his hands in his pockets, and headed towards the marina. He would certainly have some explaining to do the next day, if only she'd talk to him. He thought to himself, "Steve, you've really done it now."

Suzanne was at the shop early, slamming drawers, moving things from one shelf to another, she even let the answering machine pick up for her. Engrossed in frenetic activity, Roger left her alone, reasoning that he would simply let her vent, and, hopefully, before the day was over, she'd be back to normal. He had to admit that he had never seen his boss this way before, and, if he knew what to do for her, he would have gladly done it.

Steve entered the antique store promptly at nine, when it opened. Suzanne was in the back, peeked out and saw him, and quickly left by the back door telling Roger to handle him, she was going to the beauty parlor.

Dejected, Steve had to leave in order to not be late for his meeting with Mark and Jean Roberts. He told Roger he would try again after lunch, and left.

Arriving in Baylors Point a scant 20 minutes later, he pulled up to the Roberts' vast, three level home. Sitting on a bluff overlooking the ocean, the house reminded Steve of an unfurled sheet with its sloping roof and wavy shaped pool house. The Roberts were on the back patio when the maid brought him through the house out to the back. Drinks and light canapés were on the umbrella table, and the doctor and his wife were in matching short sets. Mark got up to shake Steve's hand as he approached.

"Thomas, good to see you again. You remember my wife, Jean, have a seat, won't you? Drink?"

"Mark, Jean, it's always good to see you. No thanks on the drink, I will have an honest coke if you have one."

While Mark fixed his soft drink, Steve proceeded to tell the couple of the plans for the Murdoch Mansion restoration. He finished up with a plea for funding. "Look, folks, I'll be honest with you, we need money, that's why I'm contacting so many people here in Pykes County for help. There has never been a cultural arts center here in this part of the coast. We have a wealth of history and arts here, and no way to showcase it. My plan is to rebuild the house, using it as an arts center, and, eventually opening a small school of the arts here in the Cove. Think of the people it will attract, and the artisans. We might even be able to have an artist in residence, that sort of thing. If we can restore the grounds, we can have picnic areas, a memorial garden, maybe dedicated to the Murdochs, and perhaps even a monument to an unknown mariner. Of course, I have someone in mind to be curator, someone extremely qualified. Now, my partners and I are prepared to put up $100,000, and I've written some grants totaling $3,000,000, and what we're looking for now is operating expenses, something to help us get this project up and running. Here, let me show you these blueprints." He unrolled the blueprints, bringing two chairs together to hold them. "The piece de resistance is this grand staircase, right here. IT has a broad landing, something big enough to put musicians, and from there, we can have band concerts. What we need to do right now is have a fundraiser, so I spoke with the members of the town council, and Sam Myers in particular, since he's the mayor, and we decided the Fisherman's Wharf Festival over Labor Day will be our kick off date. All proceeds that day will go towards the restorations, plus, we'll have some open air booths set up on the grounds of the mansion that day to help raise some money. The Browns will have a table of flowers and plants for sale, Kevin McLaughlin said he would do something, but at this point he wasn't sure just what. Every merchant in town is going to help out, well, there is one I haven't been able to see yet, but I'm sure she'll go along with what everyone else is doing. We'll do a bake sale, and, one of my partners is over in town in Baylor's Point right now trying to convince a car dealer to let us have a car to raffle off. Well," he said re-rolling the blueprints and gathering all his material. "That's pretty much it. Can I count on your help, you'll get a nice plaque square in the downstairs foyer of the house for a generous contribution. I hate to put the bums rush on you, but Labor Day is less than a month away, and we need to make our plans."

Rising with Steve, Mark put his hand out, and offered to walk him to his car. "Oh, I think Jean and I are probably good for $25,000 at this point Thomas. We think it's a great idea. The county needs something other than another antique and doodad shop. Fine thing you're doing here." He slapped Steve on the back, as he got into the rental car. He kept the window down and waved as he drove away, wondering what Suzanne would think of Mark Roberts assessment of the stores in the county. Not much, he reasoned, as he headed for the coastal highway and his long awaited return to Beryl's Cove. He was anxious to get there and reconnect with her.

All of his attempts to reach Suzanne that afternoon were futile. Anytime he went near her, she left or simply ignored him and went somewhere else. Frustrated beyond belief, he decided to see if Lorraine was in her real estate office, because, if anyone could reach Suzanne, it was her best friend. Leaving the rental car in the marina parking lot, he headed for the Brackett Real Estate Office on Oak Avenue. He didn't care what it took, he was going to get through to Suzanne, he simply had to.

Chapter Twenty - One

Coldwell Antiques opened promptly at nine the next morning, and customers started coming in shortly thereafter. Late summer tourist business was good, and Suzanne was showing some Irish crystal to an elderly couple, when Lorraine, followed by Steve, walked into the store. Since there were several other browsers in the shop, they pretended to be looking at things, while Suzanne eyed them from another part of the store. Using hand motions, and body language, Suzanne asked them what they were doing, and Lorraine responded that they needed to, talk with her.

Finally after ringing up the last sale, Suzannne approached the two of them. "You make a handsome couple, I must say. To what do I owe the pleasure, and I'm truly surprised you could find the time for me Mr. Thomas. Shouldn't you be somewhere else by now?" She looked at her watch for extra effect, all the while successfully avoiding eye contact with Steve.

"Well," Lorraine began, "I can see you two have lots to talk about, don't mind me, I'll see myself out, thank you very much. Ta ta and all that!" Three steps and she was out the door leaving Suzanne alone with Steve. For extra measure, Lorraine grabbed the closed sign and hung it up as she breezed out of the shop.

For several seconds, the two of them faced each other and stared at one another. Slowly, Steve drew her to him and held her tightly, kissing the top of her head. He put his hands on her shoulders and held her at arm's length. "There, isn't that much better?" We're still going steady, aren't we?"

"Oh Steve, there are just so many unanswered questions about you. I don't know whether to hug you or slug you. It's fairly obvious from all the buzz around town why you left, bat you were in such a hurry, and where have you been since you've been back? Do you know I waited until 11:00 the other night, and you didn't come by, you didn't call. What am I to think?"

He led her over to the two Bentwood rocking chairs in the front of the store, and seating her in one, he took the other and drew it up next to hers. They began to rock in tandem, all the while he held tight to her hand. No way he thought was he ever letting her go again. "Well, you see," he said, "That's where you're wrong. I did come by, after you were asleep, and I threw a stone up at your window, but you didn't respond. Guess you didn't hear it."

"Oh I heard it all right, me and Elvis. I just didn't feel like being nice to you right then."

They continued to rock, Steve enfolding her hand now with both of his.

"I was on a deadline. Look, seeing how much the mansion meant to this town, I e mailed M.J. to check out the grant money that's available for restoration purposes, and also asked her to do some research on the house, the whole town really. She mailed back several days later saying the National Foundation of Historical Restoration had some grant money, and she would begin working on it right away. Of course, there was a cut off date, and it was fast approaching. Cut off for this year anyway, so I grabbed the opportunity while I had it. When I went back to Norfolk, I took the grant that M.J. had written, and personally delivered it to Washington, and had a chance to talk to some folks up there while I was at it. Then, I sent M.J. down here to have a look at the place, but she had already come up with some preliminary drawings when she got here. Naturally, she liked what she saw, and now the ball is rolling. As for me, when I got back, I had made arrangements to talk to some of the locals who might have the money to help us do some financing, so that is where I've been. Listen, Suze, I've got pledges from the Roberts's, from Jack and MaeRuth, even old Sam Myers has kicked in some bucks. So, you see, sweetheart, I have been busy, but, I have been neglectful of you as well, and I am truly sorry. Will you forgive me?"

Looking into his brown eyes, she found it difficult to resist him. Leaning across the arms of the chairs, she kissed him.

"I just can't help myself around you. Of course I forgive you. Now what?"

Steve leaned back in his chair and was silent for quite some time. They seemed, to be enjoying the quiet and each other's company. Neither spoke right away. "You know, I've been thinking," he said. "Suze, I really am an old fashioned kind of guy, and, maybe you have gotten the wrong impression of me, or else I really care more for you than I first thought, but I kind of think maybe we need to move slowly. I spent many, many years in the Navy, with no time to cultivate serious relationships, and I definitely don't want to lose you, but I don't think us moving in together is the right thing to do either. Not now, anyway. Lorraine had a renter to move out of one of her cabins, so I am over there with a phone, my pc, and just a very few personal belongings, this is a small town darling, and I don't want your reputation sullied, so, even though we'll be spending a great deal of time together, let's remain at our respective residences. OK?" He looked at her, and marveling again at her beauty, he kissed her again, this time somewhat more ardently. "How's Elvis?" He whispered into her hair.

"Oh Steve, I do love you, and I appreciate your caring so much. I wasn't entirely comfortable about living together too. You know our generation wasn't raised that way. I guess this means we're from the old school doesn't it. Fogies, they'll call us. Now, tell me all about the house, and your plans for the cultural center. I'm all ears, and, from what I've heard, it sounds wonderful."

Standing up, Steve pulled her up and into his arms, where he gave her a lingering kiss. Repositioning the chairs back to where they were, he took her hand in his. "Tell you what, let's really do it up big tonight. Let's celebrate by taking a moonlit cruise after dinner. What do you say? Now, I left the Lucky Lady in Newport News to have some refurbishing done, but Sam Myers said we could use his boat tonight. Just for a little while, we'll talk then. How does that sound?"

Suzanne was visibly impressed. "Sam Myers? How in earth did you do that? That old geezer never has any use for anyone, much less loan them his boat. How did you do that?"

"It wasn't me," Steve laughed. "M.J. got to him before leaving town. She can talk anyone into anything. Quite a remarkable woman isn't she. She got money out of that "old geezer" as you call him, before the day was over when she was here. Sam may be difficult, but he loves this town, he wants to see that cultural center here as much as anyone else does." He had the door to the shop open, was removing the closed sign, when he turned once again to Suzanne. "I'll pick you up at closing. You stay my girl, you hear? Here," he said, handing her the sign, "you may want to put this back."

He was almost out the door when Suzanne rushed to him, kissing him once again. "By the way, Elvis is fine, he can stay with me as long as you need him to."

Steve Thomas headed down the boardwalk towards the marina with the broadest grin anyone had ever seen on his face. Waving to a couple riding by on bicycles, he walked into Clyde's Bait N Tackle shop, hoping to sign up another patron for the future Pykes County Cultural Arts Center.

Chapter Twenty - Two

Dinner on board Sam's boat that night was wonderful, and the next two nights as well. The moonlight on the water made it glisten like fine crystal, and the gentle rocking of the yacht at its mooring was just enough to keep Steve and Suzanne in a relaxed state of mind. He cooked for her all three nights, after they had decided they would rather eat on board, than go out for dinner. Casually dressed, they sat on deck holding hands and star-gazing until very late.

After their third night in a row on the boat, Steve told her he had to be in Wilmington the next day to pick up the architectural plans that had been put into blue print form. Everything was ready now for the Labor Day kickoff of the Beryl's Cove campaign to restore the Murdoch Mansion.

Walking her home around midnight, there were a few locals and tourists out at that time. The yacht club was still serving the midnight buffet, and there was lots of music coming up the street from the Dry Dock. Steve was holding Suzanne's hand, when he told her there was a really important question that he wanted to ask her.

"Over here, on this bench. Let's sit for just a few minutes, do you mind?"

"Of course not, what is it you wanted to ask me?" She hoped she was not acting too much like a school girl, as she leaned her head on Steve's shoulder, but she also hoped he would ask her the question she was waiting for.

"Suze, this cultural center is going to be such a boon to this entire area. A real showplace, and it needs someone with savvy, sophistication and some genuine smarts to oversee it, run it, and take care of it. What I mean is, would you consider taking the position?"

Raising her head and looking at him, she tried to hide what was for her, honest to goodness surprise.

"Oh, ah, sure, I mean, this is such an honor Steve, and it's going to be a huge job. Are you sure you want me? I've never done this, how do you know I can handle it?"

He rested his arm across the back of the bench, patting her shoulder as he spoke. "Are you kidding, there's no one out there who could do half the job you can. Does this mean you'll do it?"

She smiled at him, her eyes sparkling in the moonlight. "Yes, I'm sure."

"One more thing," he said, pulling her down, as she got up to continue their walk. "You don't know this, but I was raised by a very devout mother. We went to church every Sunday, and even aboard ship, I helped out the chaplain on occasion, and, well, what I'm trying to say Suzanne is this. I've been a little lax lately, but I really need to start going back to church. That Mariners Chapel up the hill there at the end of the street, what denomination is it?"

"It's Lutheran, that's because the................."

"The sea captain that founded Beryl's Cove was German, one, Viktor Beryl Waggstaff," he finished her sentence for her and just beamed, like a proud schoolboy.

"Why Steve Thomas, I am impressed. You have been doing your homework haven't you?"

Putting his arm around her waist, they headed home.

Arriving at the cottage, Steve kissed her goodnight, and taking her keys, he opened the door for her. She was almost inside, when she turned to see him bounding down the steps. Once on the sidewalk, he waved and blew her a kiss.

"Hey Thomas," she hollered after him. "See ya in church Sunday!"

Chapter Twenty - Three

The Cove was in a frenzy of activity. The Labor Day Fisherman's Wharf celebration was attracting more than its share of visitors.

Lorraine was happy that her rentals were all full, even if it was, in many cases, just for the weekend.

The town council had put a large, wooden thermometer in the center of town with dollar amounts on it to show the progress of the donations for the Murdoch restoration. Counting Steve's grant money, it showed available funds of $3,175,000 and climbing.

Sam Myers had been elected mayor of Beryl's Cove seven years ago, and while he may not have been the most popular or agreeable guy around town, he was an astute businessman, and had done a yeoman's job of organizing this year's Labor Day festival. The mansions side yard had been turned into a carnival, with booths set up by each of the merchants. The yacht club, as well as the bakery had donated food for the picnic basket lunches that were on sale, and the fire and police departments had set up displays of their own. The Brown sisters had graciously put out flower arrangements, and the small Beryl's Cove public library had set up a table full of local history books.

The fishermen's association, led by Clyde McMartin had brought in a kettle full of the local catch, and were selling fish dinners next to the Chamber of Commerce table which was manned by Lorraine.

A dais, with speaker's podium had been set up close to what would be the main entrance to the Cultural Center, and the Pykes County High School band was rehearsing in the makeshift parking lot on the eastern end of the property.

Suzanne was stapling the last of the red, white and blue bunting to the makeshift stage, while she gave directions on where to put food, how the band should come in, and where all the dignitaries were to sit. Looking up occasionally, she could see Steve, engrossed in conversation with some local politician or banker, and she would smile and wave. She had stocked a booth herself, with as many local artifacts as she could, but, there just didn't seem to be enough time to get over there to it. Lorraine was sitting right next to it in her booth, and she had agreed to hold the fort for her.

M.J. Follett, and her brother Pete had come down for the celebration, but, as yet, no one had seen Pete. M.J. was followed by several men everywhere she went, and, finally spying Suzanne, she made a beeline for her.

"Hey, girlfriend this is great. Have you seen Steve or Pete?"

Shaking her head in mock disapproval, Suzanne kidded with her. "Honestly M.J., do you have to look so good all the time? Why don't you walk around with a sack on your head, then all these men would keep their minds on the job at hand. Good to see you, when did you get here?"

Pulling her sunglasses down from the top of her head to her eyes, M.J. continued to look around while she spoke. "Oh, a little while ago, I guess. Pete's gone somewhere, probably to check out the local women. Hey, did you see that beautiful plaque that's been made for the front hallway of the center? It's on display over next to the bandstand. You really ought to see it."

Continuing with her stapling, Suzanne stopped just long enough to point out Steve to M.J. "I've been so busy, I haven't had time to cuss a cat, but I'm sure it's lovely. I'll see it sooner or later I reckon. Speaking of cats, Elvis is fine." Nodding in the direction she had been pointing, she added, Steve's over there if you need him."

"Thanks Suze, see ya later." M.J. took off in pursuit of her partner, waving to Sam Myers as she did so.

The afternoon wore on, getting somewhat hot and steamy as it went. The band entertained everyone royally with patriotic music, and the food went rapidly. Pretty soon the throng of people was fairly intense, and folks were getting quite restless as the speakers seemed to drone on and on about the soon to be Pykes County cultural Arts center.

Suzanne and Lorraine sat on their respective chairs fanning themselves against the late afternoon heat and humidity. The mayor was making his speech, and out of the corner of her eye, Suzanne tried to pay close attention to the Brown sisters, but they seemed to be holding their own fairly well. I must ask them how they do it, she thought to herself, as she was just about to perish in the heat.

Finally unable to sit still any longer, Lorraine moved her chair ever closer to Suzanne's booth, and leaning towards her friend, she began to chatter away. "Have you seen the big plaque Steve had made for the center, it's really something? Got everyone's name on it in gold. Even yours, you really should go over there and look at it."

Nodding and uttering an occasional "UH HUH", Suzanne tried to listen to the speakers and Lorraine too. They both perked up when Steve made some remarks, but, he was, mercifully brief. Finally, as the speeches stopped, and the music began again, the crowd thinned somewhat, and looking around, Suzanne saw what had to be the biggest human being alive walking towards her. Elbowing her friend, she looked over in his direction as he approached them. "M.J. said Pete was a big, hulking guy, and he certainly fits the description, don't you think?"

Lorraine was staring at Pete, and when he reached their chairs, she was the first to hold out her hand. "My my, but aren't you a big boy! You wouldn't be the illustrious Pete Follett would you?"

"Sure would Suzanne, M.J. told me to come over here and meet you." He held out a hand as big as a ham and shook Lorraine's with it, burying her hand in the process.

"Uh, Pete," Suzanne said laughing. "I'm the person you're looking for, this hand you are currently mangling belongs to Lorraine Brackett the local realtor." Putting forth her own hand, she grinned up at him. "It's nice to meet you.

Rising from her chair, Lorraine took Pete's arm, and turned him away from where they had been sitting. "Suzanne, you watch my stuff ok? I'm going to show Pete a little bit of our town. Catch you later." With that, they walked off. Pete Follett's 6'7" frame dwarfing Lorraine. Tall as she was, she was no match for his height. Laughing after them, Suzanne was soon joined by Steve.

"My God, you look rough, what on earth happened to you?" She began brushing dirt from his clothing and face, but somehow, she found his rumpleness so endearing. She leaned up on her toes and kissed his cheek. "Been playing in the dirt again?"

"No, just helping some of those band members with their instruments, and I fell in the dirt, but, I didn't play in it. Come on over to the parking lot, I want to show you the first of many surprises this afternoon.

Hand in hand they wound their way among the many cars until they came to a sporty little red Audi. Looking at Suzanne, Steve explained. "Ahem, Miz Coldwell, it has come to my attention that you fear I am a pauper because I don't drive a car. Well, gaze upon this little number, as it belongs to me, and if you're really nice to me, I'll let you ride in it someday." Laughing, Suzanne was embarrassed for having ever mentioned to M.J. the fact that Steve never showed up at her door in a car. With his grin intact, he then led her back to where the day's festivities had just ended. "Come over here, I want to show you something else." Still holding her hand, he walked her over to where a copy of the blueprints for the mansion were encased in an outdoor display area in front of the dais. Steve peered at them for awhile, before pointing to what would be the second floor landing.

"Look here," he took her finger and put it on the same spot. "Right here, outside what will be your office is this big landing, and in it will be that yellow, Victorian sofa you have always liked."

Suzanne shook her head at him. "Oh honey, someone bought that thing, Roger said it was someone in virgin.......... wait a minute, that was you?" She began to laugh.

"Yep, well, actually it was M.J., on the phone. I knew you loved it, and I wanted to buy it so no one else would. Are you happy?"

Wrapping her arms around his neck, Suzanne couldn't hide her pleasure. "Oh darling, how thoughtful of you. Happy? I'm just thrilled beyond words!"

"Well, good. Now, come over here, as I want to show you something else."

Vendors and chamber of commerce people were packing everything up, removing the unsold food, and folding away the chairs, but, the table next to the bandstand was still there, and on it, was the big wooden plaque with the bronze name plate on it. Below the bronze plate, were the names of the committee, and major contributors who made up the board of directors for the mansion restoration and cultural center. Steve picked it up and handed it to Suzanne. "Here, read the last sentence."

"Special thanks to the first curator and director of the Pykes County Cultural Arts Center and School of the Arts
SUZANNE C THOMAS"

She looked at the lettering, then she looked at Steve. Unable to say anything coherent, finally she gazed at him questioningly. "What does this mean?"

Steve carefully put the plaque back down on the table, and took both her hands in his. "It means, Coldwell, that I want you to marry me. Suzanne C. Thomas is your married name, if you'll have me."

"Oh my God, Steve." she could not continue, and she was beginning to cry. Looking around, she saw that all activity had stopped, while people stood staring and grinning at the two of them.

"Go on, say something!" Sam Myers barked. "We're wanting to go to the fireworks down on the beach, answer him for gosh sakes!"

Steve handed her his hankerchief as she blew into it and nodded at the same time. What was left of the crowd began cheering and slapping them both on the back. Finally, pulling her away, Steve took her by the hand up the street towards Coldwell Antiques. They stopped at the door, and he made a grand sweeping gesture as she eyed the brand new flower boxes filled with Geraniums that sat on either side of the door. This only made her cry more, and blow her nose again. Once inside the shop, Steve sat her down in a rocking chair and fetched a box from the back room. Opening it, she saw the sweetest looking Bull Dog puppy she had ever seen in her life. He was tan, with a little pig tail, and a white face. He wiggled from every fiber of his being as Suzanne held him and sobbed into his neck. When he looked at her, just the tip of his pink tongue was protruding through his teeth, and the sight of him made her laugh through her tears.

Sniffling, she stroked his head, "what's his name?"

"Hound Dawg," Steve replied.

The name sent peals of laughter through her, and she cried harder. "But darling, he's not a hound dog. We can't call him Hound."

"No," he said, "we'll call him Dawg."

Suzanne was weeping and crying so hard, she got the hiccups. Coming to her side, Steve embraced her and Dawg. "Oh Suze, we're going to have the best marriage, you watch, and you know why?"

"Because you make me laugh," Suzanne sobbed into his shoulder.

"Yeah, well, that too."

Chapter Twenty - Four

Winter on the coast of North Carolina, and at the Outer Banks can be brutal; cold, windy, rough seas, and not the occasional ice storm. Tourists are sparse, but, there is always the diehard deep sea fisherman with a profound sense of adventure, and pier fishing continues all year round. Most of those folks rent cottages, or stay with friends at the coast. For the most part, the towns quiet down, and glide through the holiday season, before getting started on their spring spruce up just in time to start the tourist season all over again.

It was for these reasons and more, that Steve and Suzanne decided on a winter wedding. They wanted a small crowd, just their local friends, and what family members they could gather, and, Steve had planned a Las Vegas honeymoon for the two of them while the reconstruction of the Pykes County Cultural Arts Center, and School of the Arts was begun. They planned to return in time to get the mansion that housed the center completed in time for the tourist season. Finishing off the interior would take a great deal of time, and Suzanne wanted to be in the cove to supervise and oversee the work.

Soon after their engagement became official at the Fishermans Wharf festival, Steve took off to Norfolk to wind up his business affairs, and pack up his personal belongings, while Suzanne began the work of putting together their plans for the wedding, which was to come off sometime around mid-January.

Thanksgiving and Christmas this year found them attending and hosting holiday parties, and showing off Suzanne's 2 carat ring Steve had brought her from Norfolk.

Lorraine, with Pete on her arm, had given them an engagement party, official engagement party, soon after the New Year, and they had presented the couple with a complete set of holiday glassware and Christmas china. Soon after the party, Steve had left again for his Virginia home to sign the papers on the sale of his condo, and to give M.J. Power of Attorney for their shared business interests. He was due back in the Cove within a matter of days, and, Suzanne and Lorraine were frantically searching out a wedding dress for Suzanne during his absence.

Coming home from another day of shopping, they walked into the kitchen of the Coldwell cottage, only to be greeted by Elvis and Hound Dawg, who had grown considerably in the past several months. Chasing each other through the small house made for quite a scene, and the two women laughed as the pets circled round and round in a futile effort to catch and attack one another.

"Just look at that," Lorraine laughed, "those two don't have a lick of sense, and that cat is ridiculous Suzanne. Look at him hunch up as if to scare that bull dog! It's laughable!"

Sensing audience attention, the two animals scampered up the stairs, hissing and growling, only to fall asleep against one another on Suzanne's bed.

"Yeah, they're cute all right, just like having a couple toddlers under foot. They are company though, you know?" Handing her friend a cup of coffee, the women headed for Suzanne's living room, and the comfort of the big, plump sofa.

"Well, Suze, we've looked in every store in the tri county area, we are either going to have to go farther afield, such as in New Bern or Wilmington, or you will have to decide about one of the dresses you've already tried on. Personally, I liked that cream colored satin suit we saw in Dillards, I thought it looked ravishing on you, and the color is perfect for a winter wedding."

Suzanne put her cup on the coffee table "Hm, I don't know Rainey, it was pretty, but so tailored and stiff looking. I am more a casual type person. I really need something a little less binding perhaps. Think I'll wait until Steve gets back, and maybe he and I can go foraging somewhere."

Sighing, Lorraine eyed her friend appreciatively, "Girlfriend, I can't get my dress till you decide on a style. Didn't anything appeal to you today?"

Just as Suzanne was about to answer her, the doorbell rang. With a shrug of her shoulders, she went to the door, only to return with the Brown sisters in tow, Harriette carrying a large, suitbox.

"Harriette, put the box down, so we can show Suzanne what we've got," Edna instructed. "Now you girls sit down, Harriette and I want to show you something."

Harriette nodded as she unwrapped the box for Suzanne. Out came the most beautiful confection Suzanne had ever seen. The sweetest, Victorian styled dress, all lace and organza and ribbon. High waist, mutton sleeves, exactly what she had been looking for. Lying next to it was a beautiful cloche.

Holding it up to herself, Suzanne gasped, "Oh my, where did you get this, it's stunning!"

Edna Brown beamed as she gazed at her friend, "well, sister and I wanted you to have it, if you will, it was to have been my wedding dress."

"Yes, wedding dress," Harriette added. "Sister lost her beau in the war, you know, so we packed it away, never been out of this box. Do you like it?"

"Like it, I love it, it's perfect! Miz Edna, I never knew you were engaged to be married. How awful for you to have lost him." Suzanne touched Edna Browns arm and smiled at her. She still had much to learn about these Cove people she had been away from for so long a time.

Twirling around to show off the dress, the women laughed and smiled approvingly. Lorraine was beside herself with glee, and the Browns just glowed with happiness. Laying the dress carefully over the back of a chair, Suzanne motioned for them all to sit down.

"Now, tell me about this beau of yours, and what happened to him. Lorraine, how bout fixing us all some coffee, Harriette, you sit down to and listen to Edna."

Fluttering her hands, and giving in to a chaste blush, Edna leaned back in her chair. "Well, it was a long time ago, everyone was called up for the war, and, he went as well. Just a young man from school I had been keeping company with, his name was Lawrence, Larry, we called him. Larry Evans. His daddy was a commercial fisherman, Larry was an only child, but, despite that, he was still accepted when he went to sign up. He wasn't really called up, volunteered he did..."

"Yes, volunteered," Harriette added.

"Anyway," Edna continued, "we decided to get married when he got home, only, and he never came home. Died on Normandy beach he did." Edna sighed, and looked wistfully at her beloved sister. "Well, no matter, I had found this dress over in Baylors Point one day and just kept it wrapped up until word came to us about Larry, then, I had it sealed in this box, but, if you would like to wear it Suzanne, I am more than happy to give it to you. In fact, I insist. I was your size once, so it shouldn't need too much altering."

Obviously touched beyond words, Suzanne could only nod. Rising, she walked over to Edna Brown and embraced her old friend.

"Oh Edna, I don't know what to say, I am just so touched and grateful to you, Lorraine and I have looked in every store here, Baylors Point, and Pykes Bay, but, I haven't found anything I love as much as this beautiful dress. Truly I am honored, and I can't thank you enough, and that lovely ivory color is just perfect for a winter wedding, don't you think so Rainey?"

Smiling at her friend, Lorraine nodded, "Yes, perfect."

Harriette arose and joined her sister as they headed for Suzanne's front door. "Sister and I need to get back to the flower shop girls, but, we just had to bring this to you. Just let us know the particulars, and we'll have the most beautiful flowers at the church for your very special day, won't we sister?"

"Yes, beautiful flowers, the loveliest you've ever seen," Harriette added.

With a wave, the two Octegenarians were out the door and down the sidewalk towards their car and then, it was back to Browns florist for them.

Closing the door, Suzanne turned to face her friend. "Raine, can you believe this? I never would've guessed Edna Brown was ever engaged. What a remarkable story, and this dress, is just to die for!" She again picked up Edna's dress and twirled with it. Lovingly, she placed it back in the box, and headed for the stairs with it, calling out to Lorraine as she started towards her upstairs bedroom. "Let's go back to the store Rainey, all I need now are shoes, and you can start looking for something for you to wear. Be down in a sec."

Chapter Twenty - Five

Their shopping completed, Lorraine and Suzanne were having a light supper at the Yacht club. Exhausted by the day, Suzanne could not keep from yawning, as she devoured her broiled perch.

"Sorry Raine, I just feel such relief to have it all over with. Getting married seems to involve so much nowadays, I am almost tempted to just elope."

"Don't even think about it girl," Lorraine aimed her fork at her friend, and waved to the Bradshaws as they passed by their table. "It's not every day I get to play Maid of Honor at my age, and you, my friend, are not going to cheat me out of it. Besides, your plans are quite simple, compared to most weddings today, no gift registry, no 12 attendant wedding party, you are keeping nice and low key. Besides, January 15th is a nothing day anyway, might as well get hitched, right?"

"What do you mean nothing day, it's my wedding day, thank you very much."

"Oh Suze, don't get your panties in a wad, you know what I mean. By the way, you haven't shared much with me, who all is going to be in this shindig? What's Pete going to be doing?"

"Well," Suzanne stirred her coffee, hoping the thick brew would revive her somewhat. "You are my attendant, and Pete will be an usher, we only need one, there won't be that many people there, and Steve's attendant, of course."

"And? Who, pray tell will stand up for Steve if not Pete?"

"M.J."

"M.J.?" Lorraine spilled most of her coffee, and, immediately mopped up the mess she had made.

"M.J. as best man? Surely you are not serious!"

Grinning childishly, Suzanne was obviously enjoying her friend's discomfiture. "Sure, she is Steve's best friend, and she will look just great in a tuxedo."

Shaking her head, Lorraine stared at her best friend while she sipped what was left of her coffee. "You're nuts! Why would you let him do that to you, my God, Suze a female best man. I never heard of such a thing. Does this mean I'll have to take her arm as we leave the chancel area? People will think we got something going between us. You're really going to do this aren't you?"

Laughing, Suzanne began to gather up her packages and handbag, all the while handing the check to Lorraine.

"Sure am, it will be OK, besides, she's Steve's best friend, and she would look even sillier as an usher, don't you think?"

"Well, since you put it that way," Lorraine Brackett signed the check, and followed her friend out of the yacht club into the cold, January night. Their laughter could be heard all the way out into the parking lot.

Chapter Twenty - Six

Steve Thomas turned his Jeep towards Beryl's Cove, he had been on the road since early morning from Norfolk, and, the January weather along the coast was miserable. He had been cold all day, so he adjusted the cars heater a notch higher, instantly feeling the warm heat around his feet and legs.

Passing by Sam Myers big colonial mansion on the outskirts of town, he waved to several other drivers as he turned at the square and headed for Suzanne's cottage. He could see the smoke pouring from the house before he hit the driveway.

Turning in, he barely shut off the engine before he literally burst into the house, only to see smoke coming from the kitchen area.

Suzanne was nowhere to be seen, but Elvis the cat, and Dawg were howling and running through the house in a frenzy. Steve reached the stove, shut off the gas, and opened the window in one motion. Grabbing the pot handles with hot mitts, he raced through the house, throwing it and its charred contents out onto the front lawn. Returning to the kitchen, he turned on the blower and overhead paddle fan.

The animals had gone to a corner of the sunporch and were huddled together, whimpering. Steve reached down to pet their heads, and give them assurances that things were all right.

Entering the living room in a hurry, Lorraine stood with fear in her eyes.

"Where's Suzanne, you can see the smoke all over town, I've called the fire department."

Visibly upset, Steve raced through the house calling for Suzanne. Hearing a muffled sob, he opened the door to the basement, and, he and Lorraine took the stairs 2 at a time finding Suzanne in a heap at the bottom of the steps, just as the fire truck was pulling up outside.

"Darling, what happened, are you all right?" He lifted her up into his arms and began ascending to the living room above them. Putting her gently down on the sofa, he brushed the hair from her forehead and kissed her over and over.

Sitting up, Suzanne gazed up at Steve and Lorraine. Shaking her head, she sat up.

"I feel so stupid, I was taking some things to the basement, when I tripped on the bottom step, ooh, God, I think I sprained my ankle." Rubbing her ankle, she looked sheepishly at her 2 visitors. "What are you doing here?"

"Well, don't that beat all, we thought you were a goner, girlfriend, Steve and I were trying to rescue you! What were you trying to make in that bubbling cauldron out in the front yard, and, what should we do about all these firemen standing about?"

"Oh my God, my spaghetti!" Suzanne jumped up only to sit down suddenly when she realized her leg would not hold her.

"Whoa, just sit, Raine, you stay with her, I'll send the firefighters back. Don't worry about the spaghetti, we'll eat out. Stay here, I'll be right back." Almost falling over Elvis and Dawg, he went to show the firefighters out and apologize for the false alarm.

The house was relatively free of smoke in a short while, so, he and Lorraine helped Suzanne to the car where they drove to the medical clinic around the block to get her ankle x-rayed and wrapped. It was then that the 3 of them went to dinner at the Yacht club.

Over after dinner wine, Steve took Suzanne's hand in his and kissed it, something he did often, and which never failed to melt her completely.

"Hey, Coldwell, I have a surprise for you. Wanna take a ride? Raine can come along if she likes."

"Oh Steve, what a day this has been. I can't believe I have sprained my ankle just three days before we're supposed to get married. I'll look like a fool going down that aisle." Taking Steve and Raines hands in her own, she gave them a bright smile. "Thanks guys for rescuing me, I am such a klutz."

"Sweetheart, you'll be gorgeous, won't she Raine."

"Of course, but hey Suze, don't do this often, ok? I'm too old for this kind of scare."

Helping them on with their coats, Steve ushered them out to the parking lot. "C'mon, you two, we're going for a ride."

Driving along the bluffs, his headlights on high, Steve pulled into the driveway of a house under construction. Huge, the house was modern in design, all glass on the side facing the bay. Leaving the lights on, he went to open the door, then turning on the house lights, he returned to the car to help the girls inside.

"Well, how do you like it?" he asked, making a broad sweeping motion with his arm.

"It's very nice darling, but, whose is it?"

Lorraine was already making her own inspection and had disappeared down a hallway towards another room.

Facing Suzanne, Steve looked into her dark brown eyes. "It's ours."

"What?? What do you mean, it's ours, we have a house, remember, we talked about this, and decided to move into my cottage and renovate."

"Suzanne, darling, I know, but it's a small house, and, this is so grand, and it has the most magnificent view of the ocean. Over here, come darling, let me show you the view."

Walking over to the big picture windows Steve gestured towards the water.

"Oh I know, it's winter, and dark, and you can't see much, but, believe me, it's a beautiful view, and right down the road are the Millers. I know how much you love their place, and how much the ocean means to you, and, I sold the Lucky Lady and paid cash for this place, and, well, I think you deserve something new, and modern, and stunning just like you."

Approaching him, Suzanne was moved by his thoughtfulness. She was seeing the little boy if this man she so loved. Here she was, three days before her wedding, a sprained ankle, and she is seeing a side of her fiancé she didn't know existed. She walked into his outstretched arms.

Lorraine walked back into the great room where they were standing.

"Not bad, Steve, who owns it?"

"We do," Suzanne said, smiling up at her husband to be. "We do, and, we're going to live here, happily ever after."

Raising an eyebrow at her friend, Lorraine smiled. "I know just the realtor to handle the sale of your old place too," she offered, placing her business card in Steve's hand.

"Nope," he said, we're going to rent that out to Roger."

"Roger? Why darling, what a marvelous idea, I hadn't thought about that, but he has been wanting to leave that apartment over the hardware store. Yes, let's do it!"

Grinning from ear to ear, Steve bent over to kiss the top of Suzanne's head. "Lorraine, there isn't much to do, just a little painting left, and some outside work. How about overseeing it for us while we're on our honeymoon? Do you mind? As soon as we're back from Vegas, we'll move, and let Roger have the old place, how bout it Coldwell, let's get married!"

Hugging them both, Lorraine agreed. Getting back into the jeep, the three friends all talked at once. Arriving at Raines front door, Steve helped her from the car and into the house. Sliding next to Suzanne on the seat, he was laughing.

"What's so funny dear?" Suzanne snuggled up next to him.

"Funny? Nothing, I'm just happy. Tomorrow, I shall check with the contractors for the Murdoch Mansion, and then, then, my darling, we're getting married!"

The End